CATCHING HI

Tigers of Twisted, Texas 4

Jane Jamison

MENAGE EVERLASTING

Siren Publishing, Inc.
www.SirenPublishing.com

A SIREN PUBLISHING BOOK
IMPRINT: Ménage Everlasting

CATCHING HER TIGERS
Copyright © 2015 by Jane Jamison

ISBN: 978-1-63259-757-1

First Printing: August 2015

Cover design by Les Byerley
All art and logo copyright © 2015 by Siren Publishing, Inc.

Printed in the U.S.A.

PUBLISHER
Siren Publishing, Inc.
www.SirenPublishing.com

DEDICATION

Dear Reader,

I love being an author. As such, I have the opportunity to create worlds that otherwise wouldn't exist, to open up readers to new experiences, and to, hopefully, spread a little excitement and joy. I hope you like the worlds I've created. As always, thank you for reading my work.

Jane Jamison

CATCHING HER TIGERS

Tigers of Twisted, Texas 4

JANE JAMISON
Copyright © 2015

Chapter One

"You're a dick, Dick." Lisa Ridgeway shouted at her boyfriend—suddenly her ex-boyfriend—through the speaker of the cell phone attached to the dash of her ten-year-old silver Mazda Miata.

"Come on, Lisa. Don't be that way."

"What way? Angry? Because, yeah, I think I really should be *that* way." She sounded whiny and she hated it, but damn, how else could she feel?

See what you've done to me, you asshole? You've turned me into one of those girls.

Richard Molta was sexy as hell and a musician on top of it. She'd gone crazy for him when she and a group of friends had discovered his band Sliders playing at a hole-in-the-wall club in Ft. Worth. From the moment she'd cornered him at the bar, hoping to get his autograph, they'd been inseparable.

And now they were officially over. No warning. No nothing. At least, not that she'd seen coming. When she'd received his text message a minute earlier, she'd been so shocked she'd almost run off the road. She'd called him immediately and he'd surprised her by answering her call. He never answered her first calls. Not unless he wanted something from her. Or, in this case, to dump her.

"Lisa, get over it. We've been fighting for months. Hell, we don't even have sex anymore. What'd you expect? Flowers and a love letter?"

"I expected something more than a fucking text telling me it's over. Especially when I'm in the middle of nowhere, going to a town I've never heard of to pick up a stupid rock you bought off EBay. A fuckin', stupid rock, damn it."

"Calm down before you have a wreck. And it's a mineral, not a rock."

She glared at the phone. "Oh, like you care if I crash and burn. Go fuck yourself, Dick." She smiled, knowing he hated to be called Dick instead of Richard.

"Fine, be a bitch about it."

"I'll be anything I want to be, you asshole." Again, too whiny, but she couldn't stop.

"You're acting like some flaky high school girl. Grow the hell up and deal with it. It's not like we were ever really serious. At least, I wasn't."

Ow. That one hurt.

Yet had she been serious about him? Truthfully? Not so much. Still, she'd always assumed she'd be the one to break off their on-again, off-again relationship.

"You're telling *me* to grow the hell up? Are you fucking kidding me? You cheated on me, you bastard, with my best friend. Oh, yeah. Tell Cassie she can go fuck herself, too."

"Yeah, real mature, Lisa. I want your shit out of my apartment by the time I get back."

He was going on "tour" for a week again, meaning he'd be traveling between small towns and other hole-in-the-wall bars while she waited for him and imagined how many groupies he'd screw while on the road. "Fuck you. I'll get my stuff out of your apartment when I damn well want."

How could she have been so blind that she hadn't seen her boyfriend and her now ex-best friend hooking up? Right under her nose. Hell, probably even doing it in their bed. Cassie had a spare key to Richard's apartment in case of emergencies. An emergency like needing to fuck Lisa's boyfriend while she was slinging drinks at a crappy bar. She'd saved all her tips, helping Richard pay his rent.

I'm such an idiot!

At least she and Richard had never lived together. He'd said it would damage his image as a rocker. What a load of shit. But she'd never pushed to move in. More than likely, she'd sensed they'd never last. He had a toothbrush and a few clothes at her place, but nothing that couldn't get picked up in a matter of minutes. Or tossed to the curb once she got home.

"I never meant to hurt you, Lisa."

Anger and hurt mixed, blurring her vision. "Oh, sure. You and Cassie just fell into bed together by accident. Damn, I hate it when that shit happens."

"I'm sorry, but it's the way it is. We were kind of hoping you'd understand. We couldn't help ourselves. No one can fight true love."

She gripped the steering wheel so hard it wouldn't have surprised her to see dents form where her fingers were. "Gee, I'm sorry to disappoint you. True love, huh? I thought that's what you said we had."

His silence said more than his words ever could have.

"And I'm not going to pick up your stupid rock, either."

"It's not a rock, it's—"

"Fuck off, Dick!" She ended the call. If she didn't, she'd throw the phone out the window.

Tears streamed down her cheeks faster than she could wipe them away. What had gone wrong? Had it been the pregnancy? Should she have told him? Had Cassie? Had her so-called best friend spilled her secret, hoping he'd freak out and dump her? Was that why he'd ended things?

When she'd first found out she was pregnant, she'd been scared to death and yet thrilled all at the same time. But that was right before she'd overheard Richard laughing with his friends. They'd made fun of one of his other friends having to get married because his girlfriend was pregnant. Richard had declared loud enough for everyone to hear. He never wanted any kids of his own.

Lisa placed a hand on her flat abdomen. The week after that, she'd had a lot of pain and had passed a blob of something into the toilet. The next day, her doctor had told her she'd lost the baby.

Had the baby heard Richard and known his father didn't want him? It was a silly idea, but one she couldn't shake.

Until she'd found out she was pregnant, she'd never given having children a single thought. But after the miscarriage, she'd realized how much she wanted them. At least two, maybe even as many as four or five.

I'll make a great mom. At least, I hope I will.

She glanced around, realizing that she hadn't paid attention to where she was going. How far had she driven since leaving the highway? Where the hell was she?

To make matters worse, she needed a bathroom in a bad way. Although there was no sign telling her how far the small town of Crosston was, according dickhead Dick's directions, she had to be going the right way. How much longer until she saw anything pointing her way to the town?

Damn it. I'm going to have to pull off and squat by the side of the road. Great. Just great. With my luck, a bunch of jerks will ride by and see me.

This is so fucked up.

Dumped by Richard. It hurt. But did it hurt because she'd actually cared for him or because it was just so damn embarrassing?

Letting out a tortured sob, she pulled the car onto the shoulder of the road. She sat there for a few minutes, fighting the urge to pee.

Instead, she wanted to bang her palms against the steering wheel and scream until her throat was sore. Not that it would help.

She'd known it was going to happen. Hell, down deep she'd even hoped it would. Had she been too cowardly to end it with him? Since losing the baby, she'd been the one who'd rejected him in bed. She'd been the one who'd found herself staring at him as he did a mean imitation of a couch potato and wondered why she hadn't already broken up with him. Had she forced him to end it?

They'd never been right for each other. He was a thirty-year old, never-going-to-grow-up kid in a band with four other thirty-something Peter Pan kind of guys still playing dive bars and going nowhere. If she hadn't been helping him out, he'd have ended up sleeping in a cardboard box.

"That's Cassie's job now." *See? There's a silver lining to every disaster.*

At twenty-five, she was still a bartender, but at least she'd been attending community college, working toward an associate degree in accounting. One day, she'd become an accountant and be able to earn a decent living. Hell, she'd even get to work during the day like most people did. Not that she liked accounting that much, but she was good with numbers and being an accountant seemed like a responsible kind of job. Besides, a girl had to do something to support herself. At least then, she could support her ever-growing e-book budget.

Usually a grounded person, she still adored a good love story. She'd realized early on that she was dating a musician partly because it had seemed romantic. Didn't every girl dream about falling in love with the bad boy in a rock band? Yet she'd only been fooling herself. Had Richard only been a placeholder until her real true love came along?

True love. Yeah, right. Like that's a real thing.

Maybe Richard was right about one thing. It was time to grow up and quit believing romantic fantasies could come true.

She shoved her shoulder against the car door and slipped out. Checking the road for any tale-tell signs of another car approaching, she pulled her dress up and her panties down.

If anyone sees me, I'll just wave and give them a good show.

She did her business, waited a little while to air dry, and then pulled up panties and smoothed down her dress. By the time she'd made it back behind the wheel, she felt better. It was amazing how getting to pee helped a girl's mood.

She checked her phone's GPS, but it still wasn't picking up a signal. Glancing around, she wondered if she could make it back to the highway. She'd kind of zoned out while yelling at Richard, but she remembered taking a few turns along some dirt roads. Problem was, had they been left or right turns?

"Damn it. I'm lost."

Going back the way she'd come didn't guarantee she'd be heading for the highway. Going forward, however, might take her to her destination—if she got lucky. An idea, one that was perhaps a bit juvenile yet held the prospect of making her happy, struck her.

What if she bought the stupid rock then sent Richard a selfie with her holding the stupid thing? After giving him a few minutes to let it sink in that she'd gotten the rock—and maybe even giving him enough time to text her back—she'd send another selfie of her holding the rock after breaking it apart. The idea was petty and childish, but sometimes petty and childish made a person feel downright good.

"Crosston, here I come."

* * * *

Craig Westbrook shifted in his saddle. As it always did, gazing over the land of Twisted Oaks Ranch brought a sense of satisfaction. Was there any better life than that of a rancher? The fact that he could think so after pulling an all-nighter nursing a sick calf proved how much he loved the work.

His best friend, Marrick Kinsale, let his horse trail along the fence. He'd already checked his section for any problems like loose boards and had beaten Marrick back to their starting place.

He'd gotten lucky meeting Marrick while they were both in the army. They'd been stationed together in Afghanistan for two years and had become fast friends. Recognizing each other as weretigers hadn't been the factor that had brought them together. Instead, a hard-nosed sergeant had given them another reason to bond. They'd hated yet respected the man, even though the sergeant kept sending them out on dangerous patrols. In fact, looking back on it, Craig had changed his mind about Sgt. Leftowish. If it hadn't been for that asshole, he and Marrick might've never become as close as brothers. More than likely, he'd still be in Colorado instead of buying an equal share of Marrick's family ranch.

"Did you get any sleep last night?" Marrick pulled his horse next to Craig's.

"Not much." Craig pushed his cowboy hat farther up his forehead. "No thanks to you."

"Aw, bullshit, man. You know as well as I do you would've stayed with the calf even if I'd been there. Besides, someone had to go to the bank this morning and deal with Georgia."

Craig didn't bother arguing. Everything Marrick had said was true. Georgia Gill, the manager of the Bank of Crosston, was a pain in the ass. "I figure I got the better end of the deal. I like staying as far away from Georgia as I can. The woman makes my skin crawl."

Marrick chuckled. "You just don't like her because she's a panther."

Coming from a town in Colorado that was even smaller than Twisted, Craig had never run into a panther before. As a weretiger, he knew lots of other kinds of shifters existed from werewolves, werebears, werepanthers, and if the rumors were true, even weredragons. But was his dislike of her because Georgia was a panther or because she was a bitch? Either way, he was glad Marrick had handled the contracts to assign drilling rights to the oil company.

He scowled, imagining a row of oil rigs scattered across the beautiful land. "So I guess it's final? We're going ahead with the oil company?"

"What other choice do we have? We need the cash flow and oil pays."

Marrick took off his hat and ran his hand through his long, black hair. His high cheekbones and dark eyes reminded Craig of the photographs he'd seen of his friend's great-grandfather, a Cherokee leader who had moved his family to Twisted and helped found the town.

"Yeah, I know. Still doesn't make it sit any better with me."

Marrick leaned over to check the cinch on the saddle. "Ready to head back?"

Craig was about to answer when an avalanche of sensations pummeled through him. Emotions whirled in his gut, sending his heart pounding and heightening his awareness. Lust, as strong as he'd ever felt it, barreled into him, physically shaking him.

"Craig? Hey, man, are you all right?"

The world spun for a moment and he gripped the saddle horn to stay upright. His breath hitched in his throat. In the next second, his inner white tiger roared to the surface, pounding its way up to take over. Fangs replaced teeth and claws dug into the leather of his saddle. The world lost its color, replaced by an amber hue.

"Craig. Come on, man, snap out of it. Stop shifting. What the hell's wrong with you?"

Marrick shaking his shoulder brought him back. He blinked several times as fangs and claws receded. Tugging on the reins, he brought his dancing horse under control. "I don't know."

"You looked like you were going to dive off headfirst. Are you okay?"

He considered the question carefully before finally answering. "Yeah. I'm good." He smiled at the joy filling him. "In fact, I'm fucking amazing."

"Okay, now you're really starting to worry me."

Craig laughed then searched around him. Not that he thought he'd find anything, but still, he had to look. "I think I sensed her."

Marrick's dark eyes narrowed. "Sensed who?"

"Her."

"Damn it, Craig, are we going to play Twenty Questions? Her who?"

He lifted his eyebrows and gave his friend a pointed look. "*Her*," he said, putting even more emphasis into the word.

At first, Marrick's reaction didn't change. Then his eyes widened. "Her? Are you talking about our mate?" He twisted in his saddle, searching the pasture as Craig had done.

"Yeah. I can feel her. She's nearby."

"Bullshit. You're fucking with me."

"Nope."

Marrick did another quick look around. "Then why can't I sense her?"

"I don't know." At least, he hoped he didn't know.

They'd talked about finding their mate, of sharing the same woman. Talking about her during the long, dangerous days at war had kept them going, but neither one of them had ever mentioned the possibility that they didn't have an intended mate. Or that the woman Marrick found might not want Craig and that it could be true the other way around. Shared mates between brothers or cousins was more likely to happen than between friends.

"Fuck."

Obviously, Marrick was thinking along the same lines.

"Maybe I'm more susceptible to her." Craig tightened his hold on the reins. "Don't go counting yourself out before we even meet her."

"I get what you're saying and you're right. But it's damn hard not to think it." Marrick's jaw muscle twitched. "So how do we find her?"

"I think she's going to find us." Craig turned his horse around and gave it a quick nudge with his heels. "Let's get back to the ranch."

* * * *

Fuck. Fuck and fuck.

Lisa stared at the flat tire. Had she completely run out of luck?

After driving for about an hour, she'd finally come to the conclusion that she was indeed lost. Her plan of shattering Richard's precious rock had gone out the window. Instead, she'd tried dirt road after dirt road, hoping one of them would lead her back to the highway.

She'd just wondered how many dirt roads there could be in Texas when she'd hit an unseen pothole. The car had taken a hard drop down then a bounce back up, jostling her so roughly she'd let out a cry. A few minutes later, a loud *thump-thump-thump* had signaled an even bigger problem. Her right front tire had gone flat.

Lisa didn't bother checking the trunk for a spare. She knew there wasn't one. And even if she'd had one, she had no clue how to change a tire. More than likely, she'd end up hurting herself and being in even worse shape than she already was.

Calling for a tow truck wasn't happening, either. After checking more than once, she'd finally given in to the reality that the boonies of Texas didn't have cell phone reception. Maybe she had the wrong carrier? Whatever the reason, she'd have to get herself out of trouble.

There was nothing she could do except walk to find help. She looked down at her feet and groaned.

Heels.

Why couldn't I have worn jeans and running shoes today?

Instead, she'd put on her favorite short-short dress and three-inch heels—at least they weren't her really high ones—determined to look as pretty as she could when she showed up on Richard's doorstep with his stupid, fucking rock.

She gazed down the long stretch of dirt road. "Yeah. This is going to be fun."

Would someone come along and give her a ride? She could hope, but so far, she'd seen only one other car. An older man had shot her a dirty look out the grimy windshield of his battered and rusty old pickup when she'd dared to pass him. Right now, she'd welcome even his help, but it had been a while since she'd floored it around him.

"He'd probably run me over, anyway."

Talking to herself wasn't going to get her anywhere. Snatching up her purse, she started trudging ahead.

I'm going to kill Richard when I get back. He's the reason I'm stuck out here. Even if he hadn't dumped me—by text message, no less—he still would've had to pay for getting me into this mess. No jury with a woman on it would convict me. Hell, they'd probably give me a medal. One less asshole in the world.

She stumbled as her heel slipped on a rock, but managed to stay on her feet. The sun beat down on her back and perspiration dotted her forehead, wetting the hair on the nape of her neck. But she kept on going.

After a while, time meant nothing. She didn't bother checking her phone's clock again. What did it matter? The sun was moving toward the west. Before long, she'd end up walking at night.

I am so going to fuck you over, Richard.

How didn't matter. She'd figure that out later.

Where the hell am I?

She walked on, cringing as blisters formed on her feet. If she ever got home, she'd swear off heels forever. And men, too.

The sound of crying brought her attention away from the road in front of her feet. She stopped, waiting to hear it again. Had she imagined it?

Another cry came. Someone was definitely nearby.

"Mommy." The wail was heart wrenching.

It sounded like a small child's voice. A really sad child. Still, a child meant parents, and parents meant a house, and a house meant a phone she could use to call for help. Relief swamped her as she turned in a circle and tried to figure out where the child was.

"Hey! Little boy? Or little girl? Where are you? If you tell me where you are, I'll come and help you. We'll find your mommy together, okay?"

Lisa stood still again and waited. And waited some more. Why had the child gone silent?

"Mommy."

The pain behind the word struck her, digging deep into her knot-tightened stomach. She turned toward the sound. "Keep talking. I'm trying to find you."

Ignoring the pain of her sore feet, she shuffled to the side of the road. Where could the child be? The only trees were a distance away and the flat land of a pasture stretched out before her.

"Where are you?"

"Mommy, please." The second voice was higher in pitch and wavered more than the boy's.

Oh, shit. There are two of them. "Is that your sister? Just hang on. I'm coming."

She hurried forward, no longer thinking about her flat tire or her aching feet. A couple of kids were in trouble. Were they lost? Or had their mother abandoned them?

Lisa was moving so fast that she almost fell into the ditch. She wobbled on her feet and stared at the scene below her.

Oh, hell.

Two children somewhere around the age of five years old stared back at her. They were dirty, their black hair sticking out at odd angles, their clothes ripped. Huge dark eyes met hers and tore out her heart.

"Are you lost? Did you fall into the hole?" The ditch was around twenty-five feet wide and five feet deep. The incline of the sides, however, wasn't so deep that they children couldn't have climbed out if they'd tried. So why hadn't they gotten out?

When neither of them answered, she tried again. "It's okay. I'm going to help you. Are you lost? Do you live around here?"

She was probably asking too many questions, but how else was she going to get them to talk? Smiling as reassuringly as she could, she sat down and slid on her butt into the hole. The children didn't move, didn't even flinch as she brushed the dirt off her dress and moved closer to them.

Her attention fell on the clover leaf-shaped birthmark on the left side of the boy's neck. The same birthmark was on the girl's right arm. "Hey, you're twins."

Again, no answer. The little girl wiped her runny nose with the back of her hand, but other than that, they remained motionless and mute.

"Do you know where your Mommy is?" If their mother had abandoned them, she'd make it her mission to find the woman and sic child welfare on her sorry ass. How could any decent mother treat their babies so horribly?

The little boy slowly lifted his arm and pointed toward the far side of the ditch and a pile of branches. She took a step toward the branches. Was the kid playing a trick on her? Had he understood what she'd asked?

She got closer, alarm prickling her skin. Bending over, she peered at something sticking out from under the pile. A chill shivered its way down her spine.

Oh, shit.

Chapter Two

Lisa inched closer.

It's not what I think it is. It can't be.

Oh, God. It is.

She started shaking and went to her knees.

I want to go home.

"Mommy?"

The little girl's voice splintered into her. "Please don't let this be real," she whispered.

She had to touch it. Had to find out if she was hallucinating or if her world had just taken a hard left turn. She reached out, her hand shaking, and brushed her fingertips over the top of the—

Fuck, fuck, fuck.

She jerked her hand back and rubbed it as hard as she could.

I touched a hand. Someone's dead hand.

Breathing became harder to do.

A dead hand had to belong to a dead body.

Fuck, fuck, fuck.

Taking in two long slow breaths, she forced herself to ease closer. This time she lifted the branches out of the way.

She shouldn't have screamed, but she couldn't hold it back. Not when two dark eyes met hers. Not when she saw how cold and lifeless those eyes were. She stumbled backward, falling onto her butt.

"Mommy?" The plaintive wail came from both of the kids.

Get it together for the kids.

Smothering another scream, she scrambled to her feet and dashed over to them. "It's okay. It's okay."

The little boy pointed toward the corpse. "Mommy. I want my Mommy."

Lisa got behind them and knelt down, turning their backs to the horrific sight. She had to get them out of there and to safety.

"Kids, we have to leave. Now."

"Mommy—"

She took each of their hands. "We have to go. Your mommy would want me to take you with me."

"No. I don't want to go. Mommy!"

The girl pulled away, but Lisa held on. "No, sweetie, you have to come with me. I promise it'll be okay."

Tears streamed down the boy's face. She pulled him to her and glanced at the afternoon sun hanging lower in the sky. No way was she going to spend the night in a ditch with a dead body. "Come on. Let's get moving. It's going to be night soon."

She turned the boy to the side, putting his shoulder to her chest. "Can you show me what a big boy you are? Can you climb out of the hole?"

"I don't wanna. I want my mommy."

"You have to. Please, sweetie, grab hold of the grass and pull yourself out. Help me so I can help your sister. You want to help your sister, don't you?"

He sniffled then took hold of the grass. She was sure he was going to climb out when he turned his head and looked at his mother again.

"No, no. Don't look back. Keep moving." She flattened her hand against his bottom and shoved as hard as she could. The boy clung to the grassy clumps sticking out of the dirt wall and was up and out of the hole in one easy motion.

"Mommy."

He reached out his hand and Lisa was sure he'd jump back into the ditch. "What's your name, sweetie?"

He spoke a name, but she didn't understand it. "What is it?"

"It's Tee-ga," answered the girl. "I can spell it. Teag."

"That's great, honey. And what's your name?"

"Kitty."

Lisa kept the ache out of her tone. The poor girl was so lost and yet so brave. And oh-so vulnerable. "Okay, it's your turn, Kitty." She held out her arms. "Ready?"

Kitty nodded and allowed Lisa to pick her up. Although the girl weighed less than the boy, she had to work harder to get her out. Her arms felt weak when Kitty finally crawled away from her and stood up next to her brother.

"Good, kids. Now I want you to turn your back and not watch me, okay?"

Teag started to do as she'd told him, but Kitty shook her head. "We have to help. Mommy's heavy."

Lisa wasn't about to argue. "We need to get help for your mommy. I promise someone will come and…help…her. Okay, here I come. If you try and help me, be sure you're very, very careful. Don't let me pull you over and don't fall, either."

Together, they nodded solemnly. She smiled again, took off her heels, and then tossed them on the ground next to the kids. Backing up, she made sure not to glance in the direction of the dead woman then dashed toward the dirt wall. She jumped and grabbed hold of a clump of grass. Using her feet to push against the wall, she pulled her body up.

For a moment, she thought she'd fall back into the hole. Small hands grabbed hold of her arms and her dress, pulling her up and over the side of the hole. The ditch wasn't that large, but once she was lying on her stomach above it, she felt as though she'd scaled the tallest mountain in the world.

Lisa rolled over to find Teag and Kitty standing over her. Tears streaked their cheeks, but seeing the misery in their eyes was so much worse. She struggled to get back on her feet.

"Here."

Lisa took her shoes from Kitty and put them on. "Thanks." She glanced around and took a deep breath. "We need to find help. Do live around here?"

Neither one of them answered so she tried again. "Do you think you could find your way home?"

As before, they shook their heads together.

"Okay, don't worry. We'll be all right." She came between them, placed her hands on their shoulders, and brought them along with her as she headed back to the road. Halfway there, she pulled out her cell phone and checked again. Still no signal. If anyone was going to get the kids to safety, it was going to have to be her.

Should she question the children? Part of her wanted to know what had happened, but could she do more harm than good? Would the authorities think of her questioning as interference?

And yet, she had to ask one question. "Do you know where your daddy is?"

Teag's head bowed as though he didn't want to think about what she'd asked. Kitty glanced up then looked away.

"Daddy ran away," answered Kitty.

Why did their daddy run away? Because he'd killed their mother? Or was he in danger, too?

"Don't worry, kids. We'll get help soon enough."

Dirtied and exhausted, Lisa pulled herself together. If it was the last thing she ever did, she'd get the children to safety.

* * * *

"Have you sensed her again, Craig?"

Marrick hadn't been able to think of anything else since they'd ridden home to the ranch. Like his friend, he kept looking around, hoping to see their intended mate. He'd know her once she was close enough. Or at least, he hoped he would. Yet even if he didn't, wouldn't Craig?

"Yeah, I did." Craig lounged against their pickup.

They'd stayed up most of the night, unable to sleep. The next morning they'd come into the town. They had to be there if she came through on the bus or drove into town.

Would he feel the connection like Craig had? He'd heard about the wondrous instinctual bond that drew intended mates together. If he didn't sense her, if Craig's mate wasn't his, too, what would he do? Could he stay with his friend? Or would it hurt too much to see Craig and his mate together? He imagined seeing them together, kissing, loving each other with him as the outsider. Even now, even before it was a reality, it twisted his gut. As much as he'd be happy for his friend, he'd have to give up his half of Twisted Oaks Ranch and leave.

"It doesn't mean you're not her mate, too. Maybe I'm more open to the connection."

"Maybe." Marrick sure as hell hoped so.

"You will. I know it. We're meant to share the woman."

Marrick couldn't help but smile. Craig was an optimist. Always had been and always would be. "Let's find her first. Then we'll deal with—"

A shout rang out, interrupting him. Marrick turned with Craig and stared at the crowd of people hurrying into the street. A woman and two children slowly walked down the center of the road. They were shuffling more than walking as though the next footstep was an impossible feat. The children's heads hung low while the woman glanced around her.

"What the hell?" Marrick strode down the sidewalk and then onto the road. The closer he came to the trio, the more certain he was that he recognized the children. "Are those my sister's kids?" He picked up the pace, fear surging into adrenaline.

Pushing through the crowd around the woman and the children, Marrick found himself face to face with a beautiful brunette with shoulder-length hair. Her blue eyes were clouded with exhaustion and her clothes were dirty. Even though she had dirt smudged on her cheeks and her hair was tangled, she still tugged at his abdomen. She looked regal as she protectively wrapped her arms around his nephew and niece. The children were as haggard as the woman with grime covering their clothes. His friends and neighbors recognized the children, too, and eased away, giving him more room.

"Teag? Kitty? What's going on?" Strangely, the kids didn't run to him as they usually did. Instead, they pushed closer to the woman, clinging to her arms and legs.

He tilted his head at her. "Who are you? What are you doing with my sister's children?"

She blinked, once then twice. "Your sister's?"

"Yeah. Donna Bask. She's married to John Bask. These are her twins." Emotions warred inside him. He was attracted to the woman more than he'd ever been to anyone. The electricity, the burning urge to have her, the absolute need to know her spun wildly through him. Nothing short of the connection could account for how he felt. Elation filled him, yet, at the same time, dread pushed ahead of his rising desire. There was only one reason for Donna's kids to be with someone he didn't know.

"What's your name?" Craig came to stand beside him.

Was exhaustion keeping her from answering? Or was it more? Was she mentally capable of it? Silently, he urged her to speak.

"I'm Lisa Ridgeway."

"Okay, Ms. Ridgeway—"

"Lisa."

For some strange reason, he was glad she wanted him to use her first name. "I'm Marrick Kinsale, their uncle. And this is Craig Westbrook. Okay, Lisa, start talking. Tell me what's going on."

Her body slumped as though she could finally relax. "I was driving, trying to find the highway, and got lost. Then I got a flat tire."

He ground his teeth. "That's not telling me anything about the kids." Why were they still clinging to her? Didn't they know him?

"Take it easy, man. Give her time." Craig shot him a stern look. "Go ahead, Lisa."

"I got a flat tire so I started walking." She glanced down at her feet. "In heels."

Was she purposely trying to irritate him? Who the fuck cared what kind of shoes she was wearing? "Yeah. And? Tell me about the kids."

She blinked again then frowned. "I found them in a ditch. Not a very deep one, but it was still a ditch."

Something was really off. "And their mother? Where was she? Were they alone?"

"Give her time to answer, man," warned Craig.

Lisa nodded in a sad way that made his stomach do a sickening flip-flop. "She was there. At least"—she lowered her voice to a whisper—"her body was."

Pulling out a piranha's teeth would've been easier than getting her to talk. "Go on. Just spit it out."

Her expression hardened. "I found the kids and I brought them here." She said all of it with a "go fuck yourself" edge to her tone.

"Mommy's hiding."

Marrick's focus dropped to Teag. If Lisa wasn't going to tell him much, maybe the kids would. "Where's your mommy hiding?" He stepped closer, kneeling before his nephew.

"Daddy got mad."

He swiveled toward Kitty, fear turning into a slow rage. "He did? Did he yell at your mommy?"

"Uh-huh." Kitty's eyes swam with tears. "Mommy got scared. She told us to hide in the closet. Then she ran away."

The crowd around him broke their silence. Gasps and murmurs highlighted their talk.

Marrick pushed those sounds away and concentrated on the kids. "Then what happened, Kitty?" Of the two, his niece would be more specific in her answers. Although the children were both weretigers, she'd always been the more assertive of the two.

"I was afraid." Kitty's tears streamed down her cheeks.

He took her hands and gave them a squeeze. "I know. It's scary when grownups yell. But it's okay now. You're safe. But you have to tell me. What happened after your mommy ran away?"

"Daddy chased her."

Shit. He'd been afraid of hearing exactly that. "How do you know your daddy chased her?"

Kitty looked at the ground and wiped her nose. Her not looking at him any longer was a sign that she'd done something wrong.

"It's okay, honey. You're not in trouble. Go on. Tell me."

Slowly she brought her gaze to meet his. "We chased them."

Teag, who had remained silent, started crying. "Daddy hit Mommy and she fell. He hit her real hard."

Marrick had to choke back his anger. If he didn't, he'd shift in the middle of town and in broad daylight, going against the pride's rule. "Where is your mommy, kids? Tell me so I can go help her."

Guilt hit him as hard as a sledgehammer to the stomach. He'd never liked his sister's mate. John Bask was a lowlife who was too quick to use his fists. Before the twins were born, Donna had already left him a couple of times. As her brother, he'd tried to get her to leave the bastard for good, but she always went back. He hadn't understood then and he didn't understand now. How could a woman love a man who made holes in the walls with his fists and treated her like hell?

He'd done what he could, going against Donna's wishes. Threatening John had helped. For several months, John had kept his temper in check. As far as Marrick knew, his sister was finally happy.

At least, he'd thought so. His gut told him now that she'd been lying. That she'd pretended all was peaceful in their home. If John had put his hands on Donna, if he'd killed his sister, Marrick would make sure John would rot in hell.

Craig touched his shoulder and signaled him to stand up. "Maybe we should get the rest from Lisa. This might not be something they should hear. Lena, can you take the kids and get them cleaned up?"

Marrick nodded, agreeing. And yet he was sure hearing wouldn't be half as bad as what they'd seen.

Lena Fortran, owner of The Rocking Porch Bed and Breakfast, and a close friend, reached her hands out to the kids. "Come on, guys. Let's go back to my place and get some breakfast. I'll make you my super-duper blueberry pancakes."

For a moment, he thought Kitty and Teag wouldn't move from Lisa's side. Lisa, however, bent low and whispered something in their ears. The kids nodded then took Lena's hands.

"Thanks, Lena. I'll be over to get them as soon as I can." First he had to find out about Donna and John.

"Sure thing. I'll fill up their bellies and get them cleaned up. Take as long as you need."

He waited until Lena had the kids through to the other side of the crowd then turned to face Lisa again. "Tell me everything you know."

She swallowed. "I don't know anything about their father. I didn't see him."

Her blue eyes brightened a second before the world around him took on an amber hue.

"Keep it under control, man," warned Craig.

Marrick's inner white tiger snarled, unwilling to be kept down. It scratched at him, tearing him apart from the inside out. A low growl escaped his mouth. Fighting as hard as he could, he forced the beast back into submission, clenching and unclenching his hands in his struggle to dominate the animal.

"Go on with your story." Story wasn't the correct word, but he wanted her to tell him everything she'd seen and done.

"Like I said, my car had a flat tire so I started walking. I didn't know where I was going, but then I heard the kids crying."

Shit. Still, as hard as he knew it was going to be, he had to hear. "And?"

"So I started looking for them." She bit her lower lip and clasped her hands, fidgeting. "It didn't take long to find them. They were in a ditch."

"What about their mom? Did you see her?"

"Not at first. After I jumped into the hole to get the kids, I..." She shook her head and looked away. "This is horrible. Those poor kids."

"Is their mother alive?"

Slowly, as though she couldn't stand to do so, she lifted her gaze to his. "I don't think so."

"You don't know for sure?"

"No. I mean, I didn't pull all the branches off the body, but I'm pretty sure the woman was dead. Her eyes were open and... She had to be dead. I'm so sorry."

He felt Craig take his arm to steady him. His sister was dead. And yet, a spark of hope wouldn't let him believe. Maybe it was someone else. Maybe his sister had turned the kids over to a friend. Maybe he could believe in a miracle for a little while longer.

"Damn, Marrick. I'm sorry."

"We've been walking all night." She'd looked tired before, but suddenly, her body started to tremble. "We had to stop and rest a lot, but they're really strong. I don't know how the kids made it, but they did."

He ignored Craig's softly spoken words of warning to keep his beast contained. "Where is she? The woman you saw. Where is she?" he asked.

She turned and pointed in the direction she'd come from. "On the right side of the road about five yards into a pasture. There was a red barn on the other side of the road." Pity showed on her face. "I'm so very sorry. My phone wasn't getting any reception or I would've called. There was nothing I could do for her, so I took the kids with me."

"Lisa!"

Marrick whirled around to find the crowd parting to let Teag and Kitty get through. They raced past him and straight into the welcoming arms of Lisa. Lena was hot on their heels, but once they'd made it to Lisa, she gave up the chase.

"I couldn't get them to go any farther with me." The older African-American weretiger shrugged. "Looks like they want to stay with her. Considering what they've gone through, maybe they should."

"We don't want to go with Lena," moaned Kitty. Teag clung to his sister with one hand and to Lisa's leg with the other.

"Damn, Lena, I'm sorry. You know they love you."

"Sure, I do. Don't worry about me. You just do what's best for them." Lena pressed a kiss to Marrick's cheek. "And do what's best for yourself, too. You be sure to let me know if there's anything else I can do." She stepped back, melting into the crowd.

Marrick was too confused and too miserable to think straight. Why did they want to stay with a stranger? The kids knew and loved Lena. It didn't make any sense unless…

He drew in a long, slow breath and fought past the grief taking hold. The amazing sensation he'd felt earlier was still there, singing through his body. Could it be? He turned to Craig and saw the answer in his friend's face.

Craig loved his sister as much as he did. He had to be suffering her loss, too. And yet, a small smile lifted the corners of his mouth.

Craig nodded. "Yeah. You feel it, right? She's the one."

The world must've gone crazy to have given him their intended mate and taken away his sister at the same time. He'd never felt the connection before, but he didn't have to. He'd heard enough about it to know what he was feeling was the real thing. When a weretiger found his intended mate, the bond between them was immediate and everlasting.

"And the kids?" He kept his voice low.

"They're connected to her somehow. I've never heard of it happening, but why not? You're a part of her and they're a part of you." Craig jerked his chin toward Lisa. "Looks to me like they want to stay with her."

Lisa was studying them intently, but unless she had the sensitive hearing of a shape-shifter, she couldn't have heard them. As far as Marrick could tell, she was all human.

He wanted nothing more than to take her home and make love to her before claiming her as their mate. But first, he had to find his sister's body. "Lisa, I need your help."

Chapter Three

Lisa couldn't keep her attention off Marrick and Craig. After what she'd gone through, it seemed odd for her to notice them, but she couldn't help but think they were amazing. She'd sworn off men right after talking to Richard, not to mention suffering through a long, hard night of walking in heels with two kids who'd lost their mother. The last thing she should've found interesting were too long, lean cowboys. And yet, they suddenly consumed her thoughts.

Marrick's long black hair framed a cleft chin. His black eyes were filled with pain, but he held his head high and his shoulders back. High cheekbones spoke of a possible Native American ancestry and, if not for the small scar above his right eye, his face might've seemed too symmetrical to be real.

Both men had tans that came from long hours in the sun. Their strong forearms, exposed by their rolled up sleeves, hinted at the muscles underneath their clothes. Each wore faded jeans and worn boots, but neither one of them wore a belt, much less a big buckle.

Craig was the day to Marrick's night. His blond hair was cut in an average length while his gray eyes, although filled with sadness, still held a sparkle she didn't understand. While Marrick talked, he'd gazed at her longingly, as though she was the most beautiful woman he'd ever met.

Which, of course, had to be a bunch of bullshit. Especially after the night she'd had. She could imagine how horrible she looked, and worse, how she smelled. What would they want with her? On a good day, she was okay in the looks department, but men like them were sure to have gorgeous women fawning all over them.

"Lisa?"

"Huh?" She jolted then realized she'd been daydreaming. Guilt washed through her. How could she think about how hot they were when she'd just told them about finding a dead woman? A dead woman who'd turned out to be Marrick's sister.

"I'm sorry. What'd you say?" Heat spread through her cheeks. They had to think of her as either an idiot or an uncaring bitch.

"I said I need your help."

She put her hands on the children's heads and pulled them against her legs. Strangely, she still felt protective of them even though she'd found their uncle.

"I don't understand." She lowered her voice. "Do you want me to help you find...you know?" She stopped, unwilling to refer to "the body" again in front of Teag and Kitty.

"Yes. But even more, I need you to help me with them." Marrick's gaze dropped to the children then came back to hers.

"I don't think I can."

Hadn't she already done enough? All she wanted was to get clean, eat, and then get the hell back home. She glanced down at Teag clutching her dress. Yet how could she leave when they needed her so much? How could she leave without knowing they were truly safe? Even then, she couldn't help but think it would be hard to turn them loose. In a short time, they'd managed to take her heart and hold it in their small hands.

"Teag and Kitty need you."

She frowned, taking in first Marrick's intense gaze before Craig's. She didn't doubt what Craig had said, but she wasn't sure what he meant. Wouldn't staying only make it harder on the kids when she finally did leave? "No. I'm sorry. I need to get home."

Teag tugged on her dress. "Nooo. I don't want you to go."

Damn. If there was anything that could change her mind, it was his big sorrowful eyes.

Craig took a step forward and offered her his hand. "These are Marrick's niece and nephew, Teag and Kitty Bask. Their mom's name is—" He stopped and corrected himself. "Their mom's name was Donna Bask."

No mention of their father and she wasn't about to ask.

She took his hand and, in that instant, felt a sudden rush of something wild surge from his hand into hers. Inhaling, she looked down, half expecting to see smoke drifting into the air. The sensation rippled up her arm then raced through the rest of her. She didn't want to turn his hand loose for anything. The feelings running amuck inside her frightened and exhilarated her all at the same time. Heat burst between her legs and her pussy throbbed, calling for her lie down in the middle of the street and beg him to take her.

She looked into his eyes and searched for an answer. *He knows what I'm feeling.*

She almost wept when he let go of her hand. "I'm Lisa Ridgeway." Had she already told them?

"Yeah, we know. Lisa, it looks like the kids have taken a strong liking to you." Craig brushed a hand over Kitty's hair. "Because of what's happened, it would help them if you stuck around. Will you? For their sakes?"

She was too tired and hungry to help anyone else. Couldn't they see that? And still she answered, "What do you want me to do?"

Marrick was quick to answer. "Come to our ranch with us. Stay with the kids. They're going to need someone they trust while we take care of…things."

Stay with them? Her first reaction straight from her gut said *yes*. Then her mind got in the way. "They've got to have others around them. You two." She scanned the crowd, waiting for someone else to speak up, but no one did. "Or maybe one of your wives?"

Marrick shook his head. "Neither one of us is married and we don't have girlfriends."

"Then maybe their grandparents?" They had to have more family than his deceased sister.

"They've passed on." Marrick dragged in a shaky breath. "Besides, look at them. You're the one they want. Don't do it for us. Do it for them."

"We promise you'll be safe on our ranch. You have our word," added Craig.

She believed him. Nonetheless, she checked the others and saw that they hadn't shown any contradictory reactions when he'd given his word. If anyone knew whether to trust them or not, it had to be their friends and neighbors.

"It'll take time to retrieve your car anyway." Marrick's dark eyes lightened with bits of amber. "Besides, after the night you've had, you need a good rest. Please. The children, hell, we need your help."

"If you like, Lisa, I'll come along and help you get settled. I can swing by the clothing store really fast and grab a few things while you and the kids get washed up." Lena studied her, obviously trying to guess her sizes. "By the time you've gotten cleaned up, I'll have food on the table. How's that sound?"

This is insane.

First, she'd found two kids and their dead mother. Now she was being asked to join their uncle and his friend on their ranch? And to take care of kids she'd known for less than twenty-four hours?

Don't be stupid. Say no. Get your car fixed and get the hell out of town.

"Where am I anyway? What's the name of this town?" Was she stalling? Trying not to give an answer?

"You're in Twisted," answered Craig.

"I've never heard of it."

Marrick's smile didn't reach his eyes. "Not many have. But it's a nice place with good people. So? Will you help us? Will you help the kids?"

He was playing the kid card big time. After having suffered through Richard playing his stupid games, covering his tracks while cheating on her with Cassie, she couldn't be dumb enough to stay with men she didn't know. Hadn't she learned not to be naïve yet?

She opened her mouth fully intending to tell them *no*. "Okay. But only for the night." Her answer surprised her as much as it did them.

At least she'd earned the first genuinely happy smile she'd seen from Marrick. Craig's smile widened, too.

"Okay, then. Let's get you and kids to the ranch." Craig motioned for her to follow them as he and Marrick started walking toward a red F-150 Ford pickup.

She paused then let out a breath. What the hell had she done? But she'd given her word and she'd keep it. Bending over, she took Teag and Kitty by the hand. "Come on, kids."

* * * *

Craig leaned against the wall and watched as Lisa and Lena took charge. The women were from two generations and as different as any human and weretiger, but they shared a natural affinity in handling the children.

The hours stretched from one to several by the time he and Marrick had gotten the kids settled into their home. After giving the place a quick look, Lisa had gotten the kids into the bath first then into a couple of Marrick's huge T-shirts to sleep in.

Lena took over in the kitchen. It wasn't long before Teag and Kitty were at the table and chowing down. Before Lena's arrival, Lisa had helped herself to their closets and found a pair of shorts as well as a man's white shirt to put on. Both dwarfed her, but it only made her look even more irresistible.

"Seriously, Lena, I appreciate all the clothes, but I'm only staying the one night."

Craig hid his smile. Lisa could protest all she wanted, but once Lena landed on an idea, it was set in stone.

"Then take them with you as a thank you for all you've done for the children." Lena spooned more soup into Lisa's bowl. "And eat up. You're skin and bones."

The skin and bones comment sounded funny coming from the thin older woman. Craig suspected Lena was trying to make Lisa feel more at home.

"How are they doing?" Marrick closed the front door behind him.

"Take a look for yourself." Craig nodded at the scene in the kitchen. "I think Teag's about to fall asleep face down in his soup."

"If they weren't shifter kids, they wouldn't have made it through the night." Marrick kept his voice low so Lisa wouldn't hear him.

"True enough." Craig's gaze slipped over to the pretty brunette. "She's human, but she's got her own kind of strength. What she's done, keeping the kids with her and bringing them into town, is nothing short of remarkable."

"Are you sure? She's the one?"

His friend knew the answer. He just needed to hear it again. Saying it out loud would help him believe it, too. "Yeah. She's the one I sensed earlier and I'm feeling it again, only a hell of a lot stronger. I just wish we'd gone looking for her."

"Yeah. I agree. Maybe we would've seen Donna before..." Marrick cast his sights down at the floor.

He had to keep his friend from dwelling on his sister. "She has some kind of a connection with the kids, too." Craig had never heard of such a thing, but when it came down to the mysterious instinctual link between mates, who knew what else was possible?

"Could be that they're sticking to her because she's the one who found them."

He doubted Marrick meant what he'd said. Maybe it was simply too much to believe in for one day. "Could be. Although I'd like to think they came together for a reason. That she was on that road so she'd be there to help them."

"I guess anything's possible."

Craig had his own grief to deal with but Marrick's had to be worse. Although he'd always thought of Donna as his sister, too, Marrick had the added guilt that came from not having protected her.

The silence that followed was telling.

"We need to get moving. I don't want Donna out there another night…" Marrick shook his head then pulled his body straight, his expression determined. "It had to be John."

"Yeah. No doubt. Don't worry, man. We'll find him and make him pay."

"Damn straight we will." Marrick's dark eyes flared with amber. "I get first shot at him, understood?"

"Agreed."

Marrick turned toward the door. "Let's find my sister and bring her home."

"Will do." Craig turned toward the women and the kids. "We're going to—"

As terrible as he felt, the sizzle he felt when Lisa's gaze met his sent a rush of excitement through him. He had to force himself to remember what he'd planned on saying. "We'll be back as soon as we can, but it might be late. Make yourself at home, Lisa. Anything you need or want is yours."

"Can you find my car? I mean, after?"

"Yeah. We'll get someone to fix your tire then bring it here."

"Okay."

He and Marrick had waited for her arrival for so long. They'd talked about how it would be, but they never would've dreamt she'd come into their lives the way she had. Still, she'd arrived and that alone would get them through the rest of the day. He lifted his hand in farewell, and then turned and left.

Following the directions Lisa had given them, it didn't take long for them to find the ditch. Craig's heart went out to Marrick. Every step that brought them closer to his dead sister was like walking a mile through hell. At last, they stood at the edge of the hole where Donna's body lay partially hidden by branches.

"Damn him to hell and back."

He turned to Marrick. "Let me take care of her. You don't have to see this."

"Yeah, I do. I need to know what that bastard did to her." Marrick jumped into the hole and started pulling the debris off his sister.

Craig got beside him, determined to do whatever he could to help his friend. Even with their inner tigers giving them added strength and courage, taking care of Donna's body would be nothing short of torture. He tugged on the branches, exposing her face.

Aw, shit.

She'd been beaten. Old bruises mixed with recent ones on her face. He reached down and closed her eyes, hoping to spare Marrick from having to see her glassy eyed stare.

Marrick stepped back and fell against the wall of the hole. "I'm going to rip his throat out. I swear with everything I am, he's going to pay for what he did."

"And I'll help you do it." Craig kept pulling off the branches. If it was the last thing he ever did, he'd find justice for his grieving friend.

* * * *

Lifeless eyes stared up at Lisa, beseeching her to help.

I can't. There's nothing I can do for you.

The sounds of crying turned her toward the two small children huddled in the corner of the hole. The girl's gaze met hers, pleading and filled with terror.

"Help her. Please. Help our mommy."

I'm sorry. It's too late.

"Then save us. Please."

Yes.

She moved toward the children. She wasn't sure how, but she'd help them.

The girl looked up toward the top of the ditch, her eyes widening. In the next moment, someone, something reached down and grabbed the girl.

No!

Lisa reached for her, but it was as though the child had vanished into thin air. Where had she gone? What had taken her?

The boy tried to run toward her. His scream split the air as the terror in the night took him, too.

No. Don't do it. Don't look up.

Although knowing that this time she would see something awful, she slowly lifted her gaze toward the edge of the hole.

Hate-filled amber eyes met hers. A low growl reverberated on the air.

No! Stay away from me!

Lisa woke up, sitting straight up in bed.

Where am I?

She searched the room, able to see only by the bright moonlight sifting through the gauzy drapes.

I'm in the ranch home.

Home? No. Not my home.

House. Yes. House. It's not my home.

She'd gone to bed as soon as Teag and Kitty had fallen asleep. Lena had promised to stay until Marrick and Craig came back. Had they returned?

Her heart still pounded as images of the nightmare slowly faded away. She had no doubt it had been brought on by the events of the past day, but that still didn't make it easier to put it aside.

The moon hung outside her window, casting shadows over her room. She lay back down, hoping to find sleep again, but knew it wouldn't come. Her heart might not be pounding as hard as it had been, but relaxing enough to fall asleep again wouldn't happen.

She threw back the comforter and padded on bare feet to the window. The latest drought had hit the land hard, but she still found it awe-inspiring. Even a city girl could appreciate the beauty of the Texas landscape.

Leaning against the window frame, she studied the scene. A pasture spread out before her going as far as she could see. Trees dotted the area surrounding what she would've called the backyard. An older grill rested on a cement slab along with a picnic table, but what really caught her eye was her car parked toward the other side of the house. The men had kept their promise to retrieve her car and fix the flat.

I can leave in the morning. She glanced at the clock on the nightstand. *Four a.m. I can leave today.*

She paused, staring at the brightly lit numbers. After everything she'd been through, shouldn't she be happy at the idea of going home? Yet, she wasn't. What did she have to look forward to? A job she hated, a scumbag of an ex-boyfriend, and a traitorous girlfriend. If she had the cash to do so, she'd pack up and get a fresh start in a whole new city.

Yeah. If only I had the money to make the move.

A flash of white caught her attention before it disappeared into one of the groups of bushes. She leaned closer to the window, pressing her hands against the glass.

What was that?

A cottontail?

But no. Whatever she'd seen was much bigger.

Maybe it was the white tail of a deer.

Still not big enough.

She frowned. What other kinds of animals had white on them? She assumed lots, but how many were so big?

Another quick glimpse of white came and went, but this time she caught a glimmer of black on top of the white. She squinted, determined to make out the animal.

Several minutes passed. She was about to give up when she saw another, bigger area of white and black.

It has stripes. Like a zebra.

Do donkeys ever have stripes? Or horses?

Her breath caught in her throat when the next large piece of white became visible between bushes. Whatever it was had stopped.

And then it turned to face her. She sucked in a hard breath.

What the hell?

A wide face filled with black stripes on white fur had gleaming amber eyes. The animal met her gaze.

She'd never seen one in real life, but she'd seen enough on television to know what it was. As crazy as it seemed, she was staring at a white tiger.

Where would a white tiger come from?

She stared harder, willing her eyesight to be better. If only she had a pair of binoculars…

"Marrick."

Startled, it took her a minute to realize that Craig's whisper came from below her. He had to be standing on the back deck.

Was Marrick in the yard? Did Craig see the tiger?

She had to warn them without scaring off the tiger. If the animal didn't stay, they'd never believe her.

She whirled around and raced to the bedroom door. Her pulse kept rhythm with the sound of her footsteps as she hurried down the stairs to the first floor. She dashed through the living room and into the kitchen. Skidding to a stop, she put her hand on the door leading to the backyard.

Quiet. Don't frighten the animal away. Or startle Craig.

As if either one of the strong beasts could ever be afraid of her.

Taking care to do it as quietly as possible, she tugged the door open and slipped outside. The slight breeze brought goose bumps to her legs and arms.

"Is everything all right?" Craig sat on a long bench pushed up against the wall.

She glanced around, praying the tiger wouldn't catch them by surprise. "Did you see it?"

He jerked his gaze toward the bushes where she'd seen the tiger. "Did I see what?"

She was so stunned by his blatant lie that her mouth fell open. "You did, didn't you?"

"What are you talking about?"

Why was he lying? "The white tiger. Don't tell me you didn't see it. You gave yourself away when you glanced in the right direction."

"Hey, what's going on?"

She let out a small yelp then checked the bushes to see if Marrick coming out the door had spurred the tiger into action, but she couldn't see anything. Had it already run off? Pointing toward the bushes, she watched carefully as she told them what she suspected they already knew.

"There's a white tiger in the bushes."

She studied their carefully controlled expressions.

"A white tiger? You mean like those in Africa?" asked Marrick.

"I'm not sure, but aren't they in Asia?"

Marrick shrugged. "The only ones I've ever seen were in Las Vegas."

Why are they ignoring what I said? And how the hell did Marrick come from inside the house? She would've sworn Marrick had been in the yard when Craig had whispered to him. He could've snuck around to the front of the house, but why would he go the long way around?

"You saw it." She pointed at Craig. "I don't know why you're pretending like you didn't, but you are."

Craig plastered on the most sincere expression she'd ever seen. And the fakest one, too. "Lisa, I don't know what you're talking about. Are you telling us there's a big animal in the bushes?" He stood, joining Marrick at the end of the deck, acting as though they were trying their best to see what she'd seen.

"I don't see anything, babe."

"I know you saw it, Craig."

"I'm sorry, but I didn't. Could it have been a coyote? Maybe a wolf?"

He was placating her while Marrick stood by and stared into the darkness.

"I know the difference between a coyote, a wolf, and a huge white tiger. This thing was three, four, maybe even five times the size of large wolf. I saw its face and I saw its eyes. It had big, glowing amber eyes."

They regarded her, their faces solemn, as though they were trying to figure out if she was delusional. She ground her teeth together. "Fine. Don't admit it."

"Lisa, you've had one hell of a hard day. Maybe you need to get more rest." Marrick's dark eyes scanned her body and, for the first time, his demeanor changed.

She heated under his scrutiny. Just as she was sure that Craig had seen the tiger, she was sure Marrick wanted her. Her body came alive even more than before, her mouth watering as the space between her legs grew wet, too. The wild sizzle she'd felt before burned through her. She grew hot even as the breeze continued to chill her.

"Did you find her?" She'd needed to change the subject, but as soon as the words were out, she wished she'd kept quiet.

Marrick looked as though she'd kneed him in the groin. "Yeah, we did."

How could she stay angry at him when he was going through so much pain? "Again, I'm so sorry for not being able to do more."

"You did everything anyone could've done." Craig laid his hand on Marrick's arm. "We're both in debt to you. If you hadn't come along when you did, who knows what might've happened to the kids."

She hadn't wanted to think about that. "Did you find her husband?" Or should she have called him a killer?

Domestic violence wasn't anything new to her. She'd had a friend who'd suffered through two years of an awful marriage and had finally gotten a divorce after she'd ended up in the hospital with a broken jaw. Lisa only wished Marrick's sister could've gotten out before the awful end.

"Not yet, but we will." Marrick turned back toward the pasture.

"There are others looking for him," added Craig.

"What's going to happen to him once they find him?" She wouldn't have asked anyone else. They'd have the man arrested and sent to jail. Yet something about their situation seemed different. More volatile as though the usual laws didn't apply.

Marrick pivoted to face her. His eyes sparkled with amber highlights. "I'll kill him."

Stunned, she looked to Craig for an answer. It had to be Marrick's pain and fury fueling his vehemence, but Craig didn't say anything. Instead, he nodded, agreeing.

Would they really kill a man? Granted, if he was the one who'd taken Marrick's sister's life, then he deserved to die. But only after a trial. And not at the hands of the victim's brother. Part of her admired his devotion to his sister, his resolute determination to make her killer pay. Yet another part of her was afraid.

His anger was primal, almost animal-like, at once sexy and chilling. Would he ever turn his anger on her? Or would he give her his devotion instead? Why did she think he'd do either one?

"Lisa, we were going to ask you in the morning, but since you're up, we'll ask you now."

She let out a slow breath, relieved at the change of topic. "What's that, Craig?"

"Donna's memorial service is tomorrow. Could you stay on and help us with the kids?"

"Already?" She winced, thinking she sounded harsh. "I mean, doesn't it take a few days to make arrangements?"

"Not around here," muttered Marrick.

"It's easier in Twisted and with our people." Craig pushed his fingers into his front pockets. "We don't have to go through all the red tape like they do in the cities. It's better for everyone if the service is as fast as possible."

What about gathering evidence to convict John Bask? What about going through the proper channels? Didn't the coroner have to do an autopsy whenever foul play was suspected? Yet she didn't want to argue with them. At least not about that.

"I really need to get back home. Couldn't Lena watch them?" Lena knew the children, she didn't. And yet, for some odd reason, she felt like she cared for them more than the older woman. How had she become so close to the twins in such a short time?

Craig and Marrick looked at her, pleading in their eyes.

"They have a connection with you. Maybe it's because of their mother or maybe it's just because they like you." Craig eased closer. "Whatever the reason, it'll make it easier for them if you stayed."

She couldn't say *no*. Not when she saw their heartache written across their faces. And not with the insane craving for them building stronger and stronger. "Okay. But for tomorrow only. I'll give—" She slammed her mouth closed. No way in hell would she call Richard or Cassie. "I'll give one of my friends a call and let them know." At least they had cell phone reception at the house.

"Great. We really appreciate it." Craig took her arms, gave her a searching look, and then pulled her against him.

To feel the way she felt was wrong and all kinds of inappropriate. And yet, she couldn't help it. From the moment she'd first met them, she'd yearned to touch and caress them. She wanted to open herself up to them, to give them whatever they wanted, including her body, her mind and—

Her heart.

As surprise registered, so did the truth of how she felt.

It's crazy. I met them yesterday. I can't possibly feel anything except sympathy for them.

Was that it? Was what she felt a result of feeling sorry for them? Was the attraction simply her responding to their sorrow?

She didn't care. Whatever the reason, what she felt for them was more intense, more *real* than anything she'd ever experienced with Richard. With anyone.

Instead of pulling back, she leaned against Craig. He was so solid. More of a man in both body and actions than Richard had ever been or ever would be.

Craig's arms wrapped around her and, at first, she was afraid he was only trying to comfort her. Did he think she was trying to comfort him?

She lifted her head, determined to show him what she felt. As soon a she did, he gave her a soul-searching look then bent his head. His mouth pressed against hers, at first gentle, then demanding. She answered back, sliding her tongue into his mouth.

He moaned and held her tighter. Hands skimmed over her rounded butt and gripped her cheek hard. Her own moan escaped as she copied his move and took his firm butt in hand. A chuckle swept from his mouth into hers.

As hard as she pushed her breasts against him, he matched her force with his crotch pushing against her stomach. The bulge against her was unmistakable and sent a flurry of butterflies fluttering around inside her stomach.

Their kiss continued, their yearning burning her lips as he nibbled then sucked on her lower lip. She clung to him as though turning him loose would mean she'd fall.

"I'm in this, too."

Marrick's growl warmed her ear as he moved behind her. His fingers slipped underneath the oversized shorts she wore, but that didn't hinder him from traveling them around her thigh to find her pussy lips.

She mewled, sinful thoughts invading her. Thoughts of fucking them right there, out in the open. Tugging, she had Craig's shirt out of his waistband. At last, she pushed away, but only to breathe, only to beg.

"Please. I need you. Both of you. Now."

Was it wrong? They were in mourning and vulnerable. Would she regret it in the morning?

"Uncle?"

The world split apart at the sound of Kitty's voice. She shoved away from the men and turned her back to the door.

Damn it. Please tell me she didn't see us.

Marrick and Craig went in two directions. Craig stepped toward the bench and sat down, crossing his legs to hide the bulge in his jeans while Marrick stepped into the deeper shadows of the porch before facing the child.

"Hey, kiddo, what are you doing up?"

"I couldn't sleep. I want my mommy."

Shame bludgeoned Lisa. Instead of making moves on Kitty's uncle and his friend, she should've been upstairs checking on the kids. The poor children had lost both of their parents.

She plastered on a smile and swiveled around to face the little girl.

"Hey, Kitty. Tell you what. Let's grab a juice box from the fridge and head back to your bed. I'll read you a story until you fall asleep. Does that sound good?"

"Uh-huh."

She took the girl by the hand. "You lead the way, okay?"

"Lisa?"

Pausing at the door, she waited for Marrick to continue.

He gave her a smile that sent another rush of wetness to her pussy. "I meant to tell you. You clean up real good."

"Damn good," added Craig with his own sexy smile.

She felt the blush warm her cheeks. "Thanks." Turning back to the door, she led the way back inside the kitchen.

Chapter Four

Lisa sat in the front row with the Teag and Kitty on either side of her. Craig and Marrick sat closer to the aisle. At first, she hadn't felt as though she belonged in the small nondescript building that served as their meeting place. After all, she'd never met Donna Bask. Still, the rest of the mourners had welcomed her warmly, accepting her as though she were an old friend. By the time she'd taken a seat, she did feel right at home. Almost as though she'd found her place within their ranks.

She glanced around at the crowd. Aside from having benches lined up in front of a stage, however, it didn't look like a place of worship. Then again, as far as she was concerned, prayer didn't have to happen inside a "real" church.

The dress she'd gotten from Lena stretched tightly around her. If she took too big a breath, the seams were liable to burst wide open. She tugged on the material, trying to hide more of her legs, and caught Craig watching her.

"You look great," he mouthed.

She wiped away the smile that followed, but she couldn't wipe away the sizzle of sensation that had stayed with her since the previous night. If Kitty hadn't interrupted them, she would've ended up in her first threesome. She gripped the piece of paper listing the events of the memorial service and fanned herself. Either she was getting hot flashes before her time or the nearness of Marrick and Craig were heating her up from the inside out.

Damn. Stop thinking about sex. You're in the middle of a funeral, for pity's sake.

She squirmed in her seat, her bottom already hurting from sitting on the hard bench. One after another, those in attendance had gotten onto the stage and spoken about the deceased woman. By the time the service ended, she'd learned a lot about Donna.

The older man called Dr. Effers who'd been in charge thanked the woman who'd just finished telling a funny story about Marrick's sister. "Thank you, Kylie, for sharing."

He cleared his throat and continued speaking. "Donna was a wonderful woman, a terrific mother and wife, and a sweetheart who was always there to help others. I know everyone will miss her. Although she was never one of us, never a shape—" He stopped, his gaze falling on Lisa. "I'm sure everyone prays that she's found peace. May she run wild and free."

"May she run wild and free." The crowd echoed his last words as though they were the end of a prayer.

Run wild and free? Like an animal?

Lisa remained in her place, hugging the children to her. Marrick and Craig stood up and walked over to shake Dr. Effers's hand as the others started filing out of the building.

Handing Kitty another tissue, she got the children to their feet and herded them toward the exit. She'd miss them more than she would've ever thought she could, but time was running out if she hoped to make it home before dark. As soon as they returned to the ranch, she'd change clothes and say her good-byes. She should've been elated, ready to get back to being a single woman without many responsibilities, but she grew sad whenever she thought about going back to her old life.

Her old life. As though she now had a new one.

She waited with the kids at the door until Marrick and Craig joined them. "Are we going to the graveside?"

"Craig and I are going," answered Marrick. "I don't think the kids should."

She half expected his next words. Half expected them and, although she wouldn't have admitted it, she looked forward to them.

"Lisa, I know we're asking a lot from you. I mean, you've been great."

Marrick's dark gaze lifted to hers. Although she saw sorrow there, she also saw more. He had the same heat searing through him that she'd seen in Craig's eyes.

"I, we, want you to stay."

There it was. Because she'd expected him to ask her to stay on, she had her response all worked out. "I can't. I called my boss and got the time off because of the unusual circumstances, but I can't stay any longer. I have a life and friends to get back to."

"Noooo. You have to stay Lee-Lee."

If anything could break her heart, it was hearing Teag call her by the new nickname he'd given her. His big wide eyes gazed adoringly at her.

If I stay any longer, I'll never want to leave.

Hell, I already don't want to leave.

"Yeah, please, Lee-Lee. Stay." Craig widened his eyes, mimicking Teag's.

"You guys aren't playing fair."

"We don't care." Marrick cupped her cheek. "We'll fight as dirty as we have to if it means keeping you here. There's so much we haven't had time to say."

What more was there to say? Was it what she secretly longed to hear?

She clamped down on her thoughts. Ideas like the ones running through her mind wouldn't do her any good. "I don't have any vacation time left. If I stay, my boss will dock my pay. Or worse."

"You haven't told us what you do."

She had the impression that Craig was stalling, buying time for them to win her over. As if they needed more time.

"I'm a bartender. I make lousy pay, but the tips are good. So you see, if I don't work, I don't make money."

"How about this? We'll pay you to take care of the kids. You can be our nanny." Marrick gave her a hopeful look. "At least for a short time until we can get everything handled."

"Handled as in finding…" She let the rest of her sentence fade away, knowing they'd fill in the missing words.

Craig and Marrick grew more serious. Deadly serious.

"Will that keep you here?" asked Craig.

She had no right to get angry and yet she was. Did they really think it was all about money? Did they believe that if they threw enough cash her way, she'd care more? She tugged the already clinging Teag and Kitty closer.

"I'll stay, but not because you're paying me. I'll stay because I care about these two. Got it?"

Both men leaned back with Marrick lifting his hands in defense. "Sure. We got it. So just to confirm, you're staying?"

"Yes. I'll stay. But only for a day or so longer."

* * * *

"Oh, hell. I'm never doing that again." Lisa was sure her rump would never be the same. How could she be sore and numb at the same time? Yet when Craig held up his arms to help her dismount, she was sure all the pain in her ass was worth it.

She slid off Charleston, her horse, and into his arms. The familiar tingle that hadn't stopped since she'd arrive on the ranch zipped to a higher level. No one could've blamed her for flattening her hands against his oh-so-broad chest, or for snaking them up and over his shoulders.

"Was it really that bad?" His gray eyes darkened with lust.

"I guess it has its up and downs." She batted her eyes—when had she become one of those kinds of girls?—and put on a saucy grin. "I did like seeing the ranch even if it was on the back of a horse. And I liked finding out why you call your ranch Twisted Oaks. Who knew there'd actually be twisted oak trees?"

"It's not all that unusual, so the name fits. Better get used riding, though, if you're going to stick around."

Maybe if she hadn't been caught off guard by what he'd said, she might've said something about leaving tomorrow. Then again, maybe she wouldn't have. She'd already changed her mind a dozen times.

She felt safe at the ranch. Safe with them. Safer than she'd ever felt.

The men would come and go at all hours, but even with a killer and a white tiger running loose, she knew they'd protect her. Besides, she hadn't seen any sign of the animal or the man. Were they right? Could she have mistaken a large wolf for a tiger? Was John Bask long gone?

The kids were waiting at the house with Lena. Lisa could already smell the wonderful dinner the older woman had cooked. Plus, she enjoyed Lena's company. Yet when she headed toward the steps with Marrick and Craig beside her, Lena was hurrying down the steps toward her car.

"Aren't you staying to eat the dinner you made?" She'd looked forward to hearing more of Lena's stories.

"Nope. I've got a date. Don't worry, though. The kids have been fed and bathed."

"Wait. You have a date?" Craig acted as though it was a miracle.

"Yes, I have a date. Don't act so damned surprised." Lena playfully slapped him on the arm then gave Marrick a peck on the cheek. "There's some action left in this old woman, you know."

"Hey, I didn't mean it like that."

"The hell you didn't," whispered Marrick.

Lisa held back a giggle and waved good-bye. "Thanks again, Lena."

By the time they'd stepped into the house all hell had already broken loose. Kitty let out a wail that could've split eardrums wide open then chased after Teag. Her brother laughed and shot another spit wad that landed in Kitty's hair.

"He bit me, Lee-Lee!" shouted Kitty.

What was it with the boy? Lisa knew some kids liked to bite, but it seemed like Teag was especially fond of sinking his teeth into things, especially into people. Even after she'd warn him not to bite, he'd do so anyway, as though she'd issued a challenge he couldn't ignore.

Kitty let out a screech and threw her body at her brother. They crashed together then rolled in a tumble across the floor.

"Hey! Knock it off!" shouted Lisa. They were only five years old, but they were rough and tumble with each other. Kitty could give as much torment as her brother could.

Most of the time Lisa could handle them. Most of the time they listened to her. But not now. They raced around the living room, ignoring her orders to calm down. She couldn't catch them, either. How did they get so fast?

A whistle blasted the air.

Just like the twins, she and Craig clapped their hands over their ears and turned to Marrick. He stood in the center of the room, hands fisted on his hips, sporting a glare that could've melted steel.

"Both of you, upstairs and into your beds. I don't care if you go to sleep, but you'd better not get out of bed unless you need to pee. Lisa will be up after we've had our supper. Do you understand me?"

The twins stood stock-still, their eyes round, their mouths parted. They answered together. "Yes, Uncle Marrick."

"Good. Now get."

Lisa smothered a smile. Marrick would make a great father and no doubt Craig would as well.

Craig took her hand as the twins scrambled up the stairs. "Let's eat before the meal gets cold."

She allowed him to lead her into the kitchen where they found a chicken casserole, rolls, and vegetables steaming on the table. A bottle of wine was opened to breathe and a wine glass sat next to each plate.

"Too bad she didn't give the kids a glass." At Craig's open mouth, she hurried to add, "I'm kidding. You know I wouldn't give little kids alcohol."

"Actually, I was thinking it wouldn't be a bad idea."

She slapped him playfully as Lena had done then took a seat when he pulled out a chair. Marrick sat across the table from her while Craig sat to her left. Craig did the honors of filling their glasses.

He offered a toast. "First, let's say thanks to you, Lisa, for helping us out. You are beyond amazing."

"Here, here," said Marrick.

"You've got to stop thanking me. I'm happy I could help." They put their glasses together with a sweet tinkle.

"Still, we can't thank you enough. And we're sorry we haven't been around much." Marrick's face darkened. "We've been…busy."

"Busy trying to hunt down Donna's husband?" She hated to bring the subject up, but she needed to know what was happening. "Has there been any progress?"

"No." Marrick slugged back most of his wine.

"Maybe he's out of the area by now."

"No. He's still around."

"How can you be so sure, Marrick?"

"He wouldn't leave without his kids," added Craig. "No matter what he did to Donna, no matter what he's become, he wouldn't desert his kids. We just don't do that."

"We?"

The men exchanged a look. "People in Twisted."

She twirled the wine, making the red liquid ebb and flow inside her glass. "I don't mean to stick my nose into your business, but why did she stay with her husband? For the kids?"

"That's part of it." Marrick took a swig of his drink, his gaze settling on the view out the window.

"And the other part?" She was pushing, but was too curious to stop.

"She and John shared the—" He paused, as though he'd almost said too much. "They shared something special. He was hers and she was his." Craig's hard expression softened. "Around here, people believe that when you find the right one or *ones* to love, it's forever."

"Even when it's bad? You don't think women have to stay married to abusive husbands, do you?"

"No, of course not. But falling in love doesn't mean the relationship stays great like it was in the beginning. Or that the people involved are good people. People change and not always for the better. You can fall in love with an asshole, right? And, although they're an asshole, you can keep on loving them. Do you know what I mean?"

She'd thought she'd loved Richard, but now she knew she'd been wrong. Instead, she'd been in love with the idea of loving him. "Yeah, I do. Although I'd never stick around if he put his hands on me."

"Everyone has to make their own decisions. Donna made hers."

She studied Craig, wanting to know more details. Yet with Marrick looking so bleak, it was better to change the subject. "Have you guys lived in Twisted all your lives?"

"I have," answered Marrick, looking a little less pensive. "Twisted Oaks Ranch has been in my family for two generations. I'll make the third." His gaze met hers. "My kids will be the fourth generation."

"Your kids?" He'd never mentioned any former wives, much less baby mammas.

"When I'm lucky enough to have them."

"So you haven't been married?"

His dark mood lifted. "Nope. Neither has Craig. We waited for the right woman."

"What about you, Craig?"

"I grew up in a middle-sized town in Colorado called Shallow Springs. During a stint in the army, I met this lug. It didn't take long before Marrick finally figured out that he couldn't run the ranch without me, so I moved down here to help him out."

Marrick lifted the casserole dish and started heaping piles of it on each of their plates. He paused at Craig's joke. "Yeah, right. The place was going into the dumps before you came along."

Although she told herself not to ask, she blurted out the question anyway. "And there's no woman in your life, either? Or kids?"

"Like Marrick said, we waited for the right woman."

"You make it sound like you've already found her. And that it's supposed to be the same woman. Like you're both going to be her husband." Which, of course, was absurd. She'd heard of polygamists, but that was one man with sister wives. Not the other way around. They were joking. Or were they playing her?

"That's exactly what we're thinking."

She paused, looking from Craig to Marrick. "Seriously? You're planning on sharing one woman?" All at once, she found it difficult to think. Trying to hide her confusion, she took a drink and dropped her gaze to the table. Were they toying with her? Was she just a girl to mess around with until their woman showed up? If that woman existed, then where was she?

"We are."

Marrick's tone had lowered, adding a silky richness that swept into her and turned her thinking upside down. Her libido took off into a wild race.

"We think you're the one, Lisa." Craig took her hand and squeezed. "No, I didn't say it right. We *know* you're the one."

She had no choice but to look at him. "I don't understand. We just met. People don't fall in love at first sight."

"Trust me. They do." His gray eyes sparkled. "Tell the truth. You feel something when you're with us, don't you?"

She couldn't speak. Instead, she nodded. How could she lie?

"It's an intense sensation that keeps getting stronger. Right?" asked Marrick.

She nodded yet again. Denying what she felt was impossible. And yet, she wasn't prepared to believe. Everything was coming at her at lightning speed, searing through her, scrambling her mind.

"We feel it, too." Craig squeezed her hand again. "It means we belong together."

"How do you know?" Were they really saying they were meant to be together? Like they were fated for love?

"Ask yourself the same question, babe." Craig turned her hand loose.

How did she know? Because she couldn't resist them? Because she yearned to have them near her every second of every day? But those yearnings were based on physical attraction, not real love. She wouldn't mistake lust for love again.

She stood up abruptly, knocking over her wine. The red liquid spread under the casserole dish. "I—I don't know what's going on. This is too fast."

They stood and came toward her. She backed away, not because she wanted to, but because she was afraid not to. If she didn't, if they touched her, she'd be lost, ready to do whatever they wanted. Sex was one thing, but they were talking about so much more.

"Don't fight it, Lisa. What you're feeling is good and right. We're meant to be," insisted Craig.

"This is crazy." Crazy, maybe, but what if it wasn't?

"Baby." Marrick closed in, taking what little air seemed left in the room away.

"No. Please. I can't do this." Desperately, she searched for an answer. She pointed toward the stairs. "The kids are waiting for me."

"Lisa, we have to talk about this."

"No, Craig. I can't." She spun around and dashed out of the room.

* * * *

"Well, hell, that went great," joked Craig.

"Fuck. You'd think as much as we've talked about the day when we'd finally find her, we would've handled it a lot better than we did." Marrick dropped onto his chair again.

His friend couldn't be more right, but that didn't help them now. Craig grabbed a rag from the kitchen and started cleaning up the wine. Marrick didn't move. Instead, he sat, staring into his glass.

They'd brought up the subject in a bad way, but at the time, it had seemed the natural thing to do. "We pushed too fast and too hard, but it doesn't mean it's all over."

Marrick lifted his glass and took another long drink. "Sure as hell looks like it to me. We'll be lucky if she stays the night."

"She'll stay. The connection will keep her here." He sounded a lot more confident than he felt.

"I hope so," muttered Marrick.

"Don't worry, man. And if she leaves, we'll go after her."

"We've got to finish the other problem first."

Craig tossed the rag into the kitchen and took his chair again. "What else can we do? The pride's searching for him. We've looked everywhere we can think of."

"He's still in the area. I know he is."

"How can you be so sure? If he's smart, he'd be halfway to Mexico by now."

Marrick snorted. "He's not that smart. If he was, he never would've laid hands on my sister."

"He has a temper. That played a part in it." How many times had they worried about John taking out his anger on Donna? And yet, they'd failed to save her. He'd never forgive himself for letting it happen and knew his friend's guilt was worse.

"Are you saying it's my sister's fault? That she deserved what she got?"

Craig couldn't get an answer out before Marrick was on his feet. His friend's eyes flashed amber as fangs slipped over his lower lip and claws slashed at him, ready to rake through his chest. Craig pushed his chair back, knocking it over. He barely got out of the way as Marrick launched his body at him.

"Damn it. Calm the hell down. I'm not saying that at all. You fucking know I'm not." His inner tiger surged to the surface. The colors of the room morphed into amber. Fighting to maintain control, Craig rushed into the living room, putting as much distance between them as he could. The last thing he wanted was to fight his friend.

He glanced up the staircase. If Lisa saw Marrick starting to shift, they'd have more trouble than they could handle. She'd run for sure.

"Get control, Marrick. Do you want her to see you?" He spoke as softly as he could while stressing the possible danger.

Marrick growled, but came to a stop. The struggle to push his inner beast into submission showed with his facial contortions. By the time he had his tiger under control, he was breathing heavily. He'd come far too close to losing it. Seeing Marrick so close to turning his tiger free was unnerving. His friend was the strongest person he knew and if he couldn't control his animal, then they were screwed.

"You know I loved her as much as you did. I thought of her as my sister, too." Craig kept his voice down, but for another reason now. It hurt him to think his friend would believe he'd ever say anything bad about Donna.

"Yeah, I know. I'm sorry. It's just that…" Marrick groaned and leaned on the couch for support. The struggle to regain control of his beast had taken a lot out of him. "He's still around. I know him. He wouldn't leave his kids."

"You really think he cares about them? I don't see how any man who loves his children could hurt their mother."

"He loves them in his own sick way, but it's more. They're possessions to him. He's greedy and selfish enough not to care what's best for them." Marrick pushed away from the couch. "I'd bet the ranch he went back home and found them gone. If Lisa hadn't come along, he would've tracked them down and left long before we found out about Donna."

Craig understood what Marrick was going through. He felt the same way. "We're going to find him if it takes us the rest of our lives. I swear it."

Marrick dropped onto the couch and rested his head in his hands. "I know." His body shuddered as he dragged in a breath. "I hate the way Lisa came into our lives, but I don't want anything to mess it up."

"Don't worry." Craig patted him on the shoulder and sat beside him. For as long as they lived, he'd stick by his friend. "Relax, man. I won't let you fuck it up."

Fortunately, Marrick chuckled. "Thanks."

"Good. As long as you know I'm in charge." Craig crooked his head toward the kitchen table. "Let's clean up then finish that bottle of wine. I could use a few more drinks."

Craig had only been half-joking, but the truth was simple enough. If Marrick did anything to run Lisa off, he'd have his head. Barring that, first they'd find John Bask and then they'd claim Lisa.

Chapter Five

As far as Marrick was concerned, being a shape-shifter, especially a white tiger, included more pros than cons. He was faster and had sensitive hearing, sight, and smell. Whenever he allowed his tiger to rise up, he was stronger than any human male ever could be. One con, however, was that it took a hell of a lot of alcohol to get him drunk. He and Craig had finished off a couple of wine bottles a few hours earlier, but it had done nothing to take the edge off. Craig had gone to bed, reminding him that they planned on getting up early to hunt for John. But sleep had eluded Marrick and he'd finally given up on trying.

Instead, he strayed to the back deck, leaned against a post, and gazed at the stars. Sorrow filled him as memories of his sister came racing back. Like Teag and Kitty, they'd wrestled and fought, but they'd also had each other's backs. Then John Bask had come along and, although at first he was happy his sister had found her intended mate, he hadn't liked John. Just because weretigers found their fated lovers didn't mean they didn't have problems. Or that one of them wouldn't turn into an abuser.

If only I'd made Donna to leave him.

But his sister had been as stubborn as he was.

Donna would've liked Lisa. They would've become fast friends in a matter of days.

Lisa was perfect. She was beautiful with her shoulder length brunette hair and blue eyes. Her body curved in all the right places, giving her the rounded look he liked. A man needed to get a good grip on a woman whether she was underneath him or riding on top.

Beauty alone, however, wasn't worth much. He and Craig had often talked about their future mate's personality. The bond drawing them together wouldn't make up for their woman being a bitch. If they'd had the chance to choose, they would've chosen personality and a good heart over a pretty face. Luckily for them, Lisa had looks, personality, brains, and a compassionate soul. Not every woman would've searched for the kids then walked all night to get them to safety. Although the connection was responsible for keeping her in Twisted and near them, he knew she'd stayed for the kids, too. The way the three of them were together was unmistakable. They were bonded as surely as she was to Craig and him.

He scanned the area behind the house. Where was John? If it was the last thing he ever did, he'd found his son of a bitch brother-in-law and exact revenge.

No.

He'd had enough of thinking about John tonight. Finding him was his priority, but he'd be damned if he'd let that murderer come between getting Lisa as their mate. Turning his gaze to the second story, he checked the guest bedroom where she slept. A dim light stilled glowed.

What if he went to her tonight? Would she listen to the primal urges the connection fired inside her? She'd started to do so when they'd come together on the deck. Or would she fight it, denying the inevitable?

Suddenly, he had to find out.

He took the stairs two at a time while still being as quiet as he could. He could hear Craig's snoring coming from his room and paused, considering waking his friend. What would Craig say if he and Lisa had sex without him?

More than likely Craig would kick my ass. Then congratulate me.

Smiling, he continued down the hallway to the guest room. His hand stilled as he was about to knock. Instead, he noticed that the door was ajar and decided to ease inside the room.

The bedspread was turned down and he could tell she'd lain down, but she wasn't there now. He stepped inside the bedroom and glanced at the attached bathroom. The door was open wide enough to see that she wasn't there, either.

Where was she?

At first, the loss of his sister swamped him, making him fear that John had come back and taken Lisa. Then, remembering that John didn't even know Lisa, he calmed down. Maybe she'd gone downstairs to the kitchen for a late night snack. But that didn't make any sense, either. He would've seen her in the kitchen or on the stairs.

Walking back into the hallway, he paused and shifted enough to heighten his sense of hearing. A sound drew him toward the bedroom where the kids were sleeping. He peeked around the corner, hoping not to awaken them.

Lisa stood next to the large bed, her hands clasped in front of her, her attention on Teag and Kitty who were sleeping peacefully. She gazed at them longingly, her yearning expression tinged with pain.

If she wasn't his mate already, he would've fallen in love with her at that very moment. Although he couldn't know what she was feeling or what it was she wanted so badly, he would've done anything within his power to give it to her.

He stepped forward then drew back up as Teag let out a cry. The boy jerked awake, thrashing in the bed next to his sister, his mouth wide, his teeth bared as though ready to bite.

Lisa sat on the edge of the bed and pulled him into her arms. "It's okay. I'm here. Teag, you're safe. I'm here." She stroked the boy's cheek. "No biting. Okay? You're safe now."

Marrick wasn't the type of man to cry, but tears blurred his vision. She cuddled the frightened boy to her, rocking him and making soft cooing sounds. Even with his shifter hearing, he couldn't understand what she was saying, but it didn't matter. Teag's fisted hands relaxed as she calmed away his nightmare.

He backed up and headed to his bathroom. The last time the twins had stayed overnight, Teag had gotten up around midnight to get a drink of water. He filled a glass then started back to the kids' room.

"Here. Let him have a drink."

He was halfway to the bed before he stopped and smiled. Lisa lay between Teag and Kitty, her arms wrapped around them as they snuggled against her.

His throat closed up, emotions overwhelming him. *Yeah. She's the one, all right.*

* * * *

Lisa leaned back in the rocking chair and took a sip of Lena's sweet tea. Lena had shown up bright and early, telling her that she needed to check in with "her men and the kids." Since her friend had arrived, she'd cooked breakfast and lunch, and then cleaned the house—even though Lisa had already done the chore—and had finally shooed everyone outside to enjoy the afternoon. Almost as soon as the men were involved with showing the kids the horses, Lena had returned with a large pitcher and several glasses.

Lisa wasn't sure where the woman got her energy. Being at least twice Lisa's age, Lena Fortran was a force of nature, a whirlwind of indomitable spirit she admired.

Craig scooped Kitty up and whirled her around, eliciting giggles. Teag let out a ferocious shout and "attacked" his Uncle Marrick, pretending to be an ancient warrior. It did her heart good to see the children happy. Smiles and laughter had been in short supply.

"I'm glad you're still here, honey."

Lisa put the cool glass to her cheek. The summer was heating up. "I hope I'm not overstaying my welcome."

"Are you kidding? Craig and Marrick asked you to stay, right?"

"Yes, but maybe it's only because they need the help." She hurried to clarify. "Don't get me wrong. I know they've got the town behind them and you've been wonderful. That's part of the reason I wonder if I should be leaving. They'll still have lots of help after I go home." She needed to get back to work. After calling her boss, he'd made it very clear she couldn't take off much more time. Not and keep her job.

"You should definitely stay. The kids need you and the men need you just as much. Maybe even more."

"Like I said, I'm sure they'd get along perfectly fine without me."

"No, they wouldn't." Lena pointed at Marrick. "Look at him. Haven't you noticed how often he glances your way? And Craig keeps his attention on you, too."

She had, but it seemed conceited to say so. "They're really nice guys."

Lena chuckled as though she knew Lisa had tried to play their attraction down. "They're some of the best men I know. Believe me, coming from a woman who's lived all her life in Twisted, that's saying a lot."

"What's living in Twisted got to do with it?"

"I don't know if you've noticed it or not, but the men in our town are special. Sure, there are great guys everywhere, but our men grow up understanding what it means to be a real man. They know how to take care of their women and their families. They're the kind of guys you can trust to protect and cherish you all your life."

"Wow. You sound like you're their mother."

Tears formed in Lena's eyes. "Sometimes I feel like their mother. Maybe it's because I've never had any children of my own, but I tend to take the younger folks under my wing." She laughed, drawing the men's attention. "Even if they don't want me to."

"They're lucky to have you."

"And you'd be lucky to have them. Do you mind if I give you a little advice?"

As if I could stop her. "Sure."

"Listen to your heart, honey. Not only can I tell that they care for you, I see how you look at them. If you three don't get together—and I mean together in every sense of the word— you're going to burst."

"Oh." What more could she say? If she tried to deny how she felt, Lena would know. If she told her the truth, if she told her how many times her thoughts turned to the men, Lena would never let it go.

Lisa took another sip of her drink, covering the emotions threatening to bring tears to her eyes as well. "I didn't think I'd like it here so much."

"We get that a lot in Twisted. What looks like just another small town is so much more. Twisted and the people in it will grab your heart and never let go." Lena's hand on top of hers was comforting. "Can I be perfectly honest with you?"

Alarm made her hold her breath. "Of course. I wouldn't want anything less."

Lena's blue eyes zeroed in on her. "Craig and Marrick never want you to leave."

Never? A flash of excitement caught Lisa unprepared. She put her glass down on the table next to her in case her shaking hand lost its hold. "I don't know about that."

"I do. Trust me. I'm always right about these things."

"Did they say something to you?" Part of her wanted Lena to say *yes* while another part was afraid of the answer.

"They don't have to." Lena squeezed her hand then turned her loose. "Can't you tell by the way they look at you? They're head over heels for you, honey."

Was Lena right? Could they have told her the truth? Was she the one they'd waited for? Would they give her the love she'd always dreamed of having? Not from only one man, but from two?

"I'm surprised they haven't said anything to you."

She almost revealed that they had, but decided to keep it a secret. Instead, she had to change the subject. "Lena, have you ever seen a white tiger?"

Lena pulled back and frowned. "Talk about taking a left turn in a conversation. Why do you ask?"

She had a choice. Either talk about her feelings for Craig and Marrick or risk having Lena think she was crazy. Right then crazy was less frightening. "I think I saw one the other day."

Lena put on a surprised expression that didn't quite play true. "Do you mean around here? On the ranch?"

"Yes. I know it sounds silly, and the guys said it was probably another kind of animal, but I can't shake the feeling that I'm right."

Lena leaned back in her chair, her gaze jumping to the men as they gave the kids pieces of carrots to feed to the horses in the holding pen. Lisa was sure she was trying to avoid answering. "Lena?"

Lena still didn't look her way. "Seriously, honey. A white tiger around Twisted? I'm sure Craig and Marrick are right. You must've been mistaken."

Before Lisa could ask another question, Lena stood up and called to the kids. "Teag. Kitty. Who's ready to help Miss Lena bake cookies?"

She couldn't have orchestrated a better distraction. The children let out a squeal, dropping the carrots and rushing toward the older woman. Laughing, Lena ushered them through the door then turned to Lisa again.

"You listen up, honey." She tilted her head toward the men who were heading into the barn. "Don't pussy foot around with this. I'll handle the kids. In the meantime, you get your pretty little ass in that barn and let yourself go wild."

Lisa was still gaping as Lena gave her a wink then disappeared into the house. Was Lena telling her to have sex with them? But she couldn't be. Not with the kids around. And yet, she had no doubt Lena would keep them busy—and away from the barn.

She's right.

Like her hands before, now her entire body shook. Leaving her drink where it was, she moved slowly but deliberately toward the barn.

They'd said they wanted her and Lena had confirmed it. Yet what would she do if they turned her down? She stopped in the entrance and waited for her sight to adjust to the shade in the barn.

Craig was busy mixing feed then scooping it into the trough of horse called Gypsy. Marrick hung a bridle on the tack board. When he pivoted around, he froze. Curiosity as well as a look that spoke of the same yearning brewing inside her came to his face.

"Is everything all right, baby?"

She nodded, not trusting what she might say. Instead, she walked into the barn, determined to take the risk. She tugged on her T-shirt, pulling it over her head in one quick move.

"Oh, shit," murmured Craig. He dropped the pail and closed the stall door behind him.

She kept walking toward them while undoing her jeans. Pausing long enough to kick her jeans over her bare feet, she started her leisurely stroll toward them again. Her nipples peaked and goose bumps rose along her skin. Whether from excitement or from the loss of her clothes, she wasn't sure and she didn't care.

"Baby, are you sure?"

"Lena said she can tell." She stopped about five feet from them.

"She can tell what?" asked Craig.

"That we have…feelings…for each other."

"We told you how we felt." Marrick's gaze was intense, his frown marring his forehead. "Did you have to hear it from Lena to believe it?"

"Who the hell cares?" Craig stalked toward her. He took hold of her, searching her as though waiting for her to tell him to stop. When she didn't, he lifted her into his arms.

She'd been with men before, but the sensations tearing through her now were fierce, primal instincts that pushed away any effort to think straight. Thinking wasn't what she needed. The men were all that mattered. She was consumed by the need to have them.

Craig carried her over to the long table with bridles and tools strewn across it. The rough wood bit into her bottom, but she didn't care. She'd welcome whatever pain they gave her, intentional or otherwise. She laid back then let out a small cry as Craig took hold of her bra and ripped it from her.

"What about the kids?" Marrick hurriedly unbuttoned his shirt, half tearing it in his rush to get it off.

"Lena." Her chest rose and fell with her labored breathing. Watching Craig tug his T-shirt off captivated her attention. His jeans dipped enticingly toward the dark patch lying an inch or so above the button.

"Hurry," she whispered. Lena had been right. If she didn't have them soon, she'd lose her mind.

Craig shoved his jeans down as he toed off his boots. If Marrick hadn't come to stand on the other side of the table, she wouldn't have taken her attention off Craig. His jeans were gone, his massive chest hovering above her face.

The men's expressions were wondrous and awe-filled, mixed with fiery lust. An animal-like aroma flowed from them, capturing her in its pungent allure.

Craig slid his palms along her legs, warming the goose bumps. Suddenly, taking hold of her ankles, he jerked her legs upward. He bent them at the knees then went lower until his face was even with her torso.

"You're ours, babe. From this moment on, you're ours." Craig's gaze locked to hers as he pressed his mouth against her pussy. His tongue raked over the seam, pushing just hard enough to open her folds the slightest bit.

She inhaled and laid her head back against the table. Craig's touch opened the cage to feelings she'd kept in check since the first moment she'd seen them. All at once, everything was clear and simple. These were the men she could never have dreamed of, the men no fantasy could ever have envisioned.

"Get ready, baby. We're going to take you and turn you inside out."

"Yes. Do it." She was ready. Hell, she'd been born ready.

Marrick's chest muscles flexed as he put one leg on top of the table. He leaned forward, putting his lower half over her face. His thick, luscious cock bopped invitingly close to her mouth. She brought his shaft inside, hollowing her cheeks, pulling him in with a moan.

They caressed her, roughly, possessively. Marrick claimed her with his hands and lust-filled words while Craig made her his with his fingers and tongue as they dipped into her pussy then found their way to her ass hole. She was filled as only they could have filled her.

Her mind floated, her body taking over. Heat surged within her as she writhed with each touch, each stroke they gave her. Her clit thrummed under Craig's imaginative lashings, going around and around, before diving into her pussy. He worked his fingers, teasing her as he reached for her G-spot and stretched her anus.

Marrick tasted so good. Not like anything she'd ever had before. She sucked harder, doing her best to bring out every ounce of pre-cum. Playing with his balls, she was filled with joy when the sound of his pleased growl rumbled out of him.

She was on fire and only they could extinguish the flame. Her hands slid along Marrick's strong legs. Her legs opened wider, exposing as much of herself as she could.

Craig drank from her, licking, sucking, driving her ever closer to the precipice. Marrick fondled her breasts, pinching and twisting her nipples. If they'd asked the moon of her, she would've done everything in her power to give it to them. But all she had to give was herself. She prayed it would be enough.

She lost her hold on Marrick when Craig tugged her legs around his waist. For a moment, they stared at each other. Then, with a groan filled with longing, he positioned his cock at her pussy and shoved it inside her.

She cried out, not from pain, but from the ecstasy of finally having him inside her. He stretched her completely, driving to the end of her. Her body responded to his, welcoming him like a long-lost lover.

Marrick got on top of the table and straddled her. "Suck me off, babe. I have to have your mouth on me when I blow."

As she and Craig had done, their gazes met, their souls recognizing each other. The burning need she'd felt from the first moment they'd met devoured her.

She was theirs. It was so simple she wondered why she'd ever doubted it.

They pumped into her from both ends. She did her best to keep up, her body wild for them, her mind aching to tell them how much she'd needed them. The noises they made filled the barn, accompanied only by an occasional snort or pawing of one of the horses.

"Lisa."

She looked up at Marrick and did her best to hold onto his cock. His body jerked, his mouth parted and she realized he was done. He gave in to the release. Hot seed shot into her mouth and she did her best to take it all before he fell away from her. His cum trickled down her chin.

"Oh, hell, yeah." Craig held her hips, keeping her from sliding too far from her. He drove into her, harder than ever. When he paused, she almost cried out, ready to admonish him for stopping.

Lifting her head, she saw his release coming in his intense expression a moment before he let it fly. His cum poured into her, warming her, filling her. His body shuddered as he fell onto one elbow, supporting himself as the remaining climax rippled out of him. He laid his head against her leg, a gesture that was more intimate than the sex.

Giving her a soft smile, Marrick wiped the trail of seed from her face then gave her a sweet kiss. "I'm going to have to thank Lena."

The rush of need was gone, but her body still simmered being near them. Grabbing a nearby horse blanket, she wrapped it around her naked body. Where she'd been a vixen before, suddenly she was a shy school girl. She was proud she'd put herself out there and was thrilled they'd wanted her as much as she'd wanted them, but suddenly she needed to get away. Needed to deal with emotions she couldn't quite grasp to understand.

"I'd better get cleaned up before the kids and Lena finish baking cookies."

Craig skimmed his hand over her hair in a tender, loving caress. "Yeah. We'll come inside in a minute. Go on."

Marrick's saucy smile struck the center of her pussy and, for a moment, she considered staying for another go. Sauciness switched to a wide grin.

"Sex with our woman and then cookies for dessert. What more could a man ask for?"

She laughed as she snatched up her clothes and hurried toward the house.

Chapter Six

Lisa woke up with a start, her hands stretching outward to find the two small bodies she'd fallen asleep with. She'd crawled into bed with Teag and Kitty again last night when Teag had yet another nightmare. But her hands found only an empty bed.

Where are they?

Fear charged to life. They'd been told to stay near the house, but that didn't mean they would. Kitty and Teag had a way of wandering off, chasing a rabbit or running through the pasture faster than she could catch them.

"Teag? Kitty? Where are you?"

Silence answered her.

She threw back the covers and dashed out of the bedroom, not bothering to change from the shorts and T-shirt she'd fallen asleep in. Seeing that no one was inside the house, she bolted for the kitchen door leading to the backyard.

They're probably playing outside. Please let me be right.

If they weren't, she'd have to find Craig and Marrick and let them know. Hopefully, the men had their cell phones with them.

She threw open the back door, saw the kids, and let out a huge sigh. Wearing matching cowboy hats, Teag and Kitty hung on the fence of the corral. They'd pulled themselves up to the highest rung and were watching Craig and Marrick work a horse.

Thank God.

She should've known the men wouldn't let the kids get far from the house. Even when they left to "go into town" or "check things out"—all codes for searching for John Bask—they'd made sure she or Lena could watch the children.

In the past two days since their time in the barn, they'd exchanged longing glances, but they hadn't had sex again. Lena hadn't had time to take care of the kids and give her a break. After a long day with the kids, Lisa had spent her nights reading their favorite stories to put both her and the kids to sleep. Had she done so to keep from ending up in bed with the men? Maybe. Although she felt closer to Craig and Marrick than ever before, she couldn't help but wonder if she was jumping into things too fast. Hell, she knew she was jumping in too fast. The thing was, resisting them was so difficult to do.

Kitty's giggle drew her out of her thoughts. Lisa didn't know what the men were doing with the horse, training it somehow, but she knew the kids loved watching their uncle and his friend. Lately, they'd even started calling Craig their uncle, too.

They're so good with them.

Finding one man who was good with kids was hard enough, but either one of the men would make any Father of the Year list. They treated the children with respect and yet still kept a firm hold on control. Anyone could see how much they loved the twins and enjoyed spending time with them.

What would it be like to have their children? Was it even possible? Two men and one woman? If she had their babies, would she know which man had conceived which child? Would Marrick's children have dark hair and Craig's have his golden locks? Would she know each man's child by the color of their eyes?

Would it matter?

She wouldn't care, but would they?

Teag and Kitty jumped off the fence. Slowly, they turned to face her. She lifted a hand and smiled, letting them know it was all right to continue watching. In the meantime, she'd cook them a nourishing breakfast.

Craig and Marrick pivoted in her direction. They lifted a hand in response, saw the kids looking at her, and then went back to working the horse.

Teag and Kitty took one look at each other then started running toward the house. She couldn't help but feel a rush of joy. The kids obviously liked her and her affection for them grew stronger every day.

How much longer can I stay?

The question had changed in its meaning. At first, she'd worried about getting back to work. Now it was a matter of longing to remain on the ranch.

I have to go home. It's the only option that makes any sense.

Her boss had called again, once more threatening to fire her. Before meeting Craig and Marrick, his warnings would've sent her hurrying back to the club. But now? The thought of leaving the ranch made his threats pale in comparison. Still, she'd have to go home soon. Not only was she about to lose her job, but she was getting more attached to both the men and the children. Leaving was going to be hard as hell, but the longer she stayed, the harder it would get.

Her heart already hurt just thinking about never seeing any of them again. Could she really stay? Or had their words been only that? Just words.

Teag and Kitty were only feet away from her when they split apart. Teag darted around the left side of the house as Kitty took to the right.

Now where are they going?

Lisa spun around and dashed for the front door. She'd chased after the twins before, so she knew all too well how fast they were. She'd even joked about the kids being part cheetah. At first, Lena and the men hadn't laughed. They had, in fact, acted as though she'd said something awful about the kids. Then they'd simply agreed.

As she burst out of the house, she saw the twins come together again. Side by side, they darted into the field and raced toward a large area of bushes and trees.

"Kids! Come back here! You know you're not supposed to go off by yourselves!"

She heard them giggle as they kept on going.

"Damn it." She slipped on her sneakers placed by the door and took off after them. By the time she'd made it to the tree line, she was out of breath. She glanced around, but didn't see either one of them.

"I swear I'm going to lock you two in a cage," she mumbled. Not that she really would, but sometimes she wished she could at least put a bell around their necks. Anything to help her keep track of them.

Taking care not to let the branches scratch her, she eased into the foliage. "Kids! Teag? Kitty, where are you?" Should she promise them a treat if they answered? Or would she be rewarding their bad behavior? Still, wouldn't it be worth it?

Damn. I should've told Craig and Marrick they took off. But it was too late now. She had to keep going.

"Come on, guys. Stop horsing around." Were they playing hide and seek again? Perspiration slid down her spine and dampened the back of her neck. "This isn't funny, kids. If you don't show yourself soon, I'm going to have to tell your uncles."

A dirt trail led deeper into the trees. She pushed past the branches, keeping her gaze on the rough ground in front of her.

Hands grabbed her, stopping her cold. Fear leapt to her throat, cutting off her air.

The man holding her was dirty and his clothes were torn. His dark eyes glinted as a sneer lifted the corner of his mouth. The sneer morphed into a smile that lacked warmth.

"Easy, girl. I'm not going to hurt you."

"Who are you?" She was surprised her voice didn't shake.

"I'm John Bask."

A chill swept over her. "John Bask? Donna's husband?"

The glint in his dark eyes sparkled. Was he happy she knew who he was? Proud of who he was?

"The one and only."

She tried to yank her arms free, but he held tight. "Let me go."

"No. You need to listen to me." His attention dropped to her heaving chest then back up. "Hear me out and I'll let you go. I swear I won't hurt you."

Like you didn't hurt Donna?

She kept her thought to herself and played along. If she could get him to loosen his hold, she might have a chance to break away. Could she outrun him? Should she scream and hope Craig or Marrick heard her? Fear made thinking difficult. Had he seen the kids? Or worse, hurt them?

The sudden protectiveness that sprang up washed away her fear. If the bastard had laid a hand on the twins, she'd tear his eyes out. At least, she'd die trying.

She set her jaw. "All right. I'll listen."

"I didn't kill my wife."

He looked sincere and yet, even if he hadn't already been accused of murdering his wife, there was something about him she didn't trust. "If you didn't do it, then who did?"

He gave her a look, silently asking her if she'd run. She shook her head, telling him the truth. After what he'd said, she had to hear him out.

"Marrick did."

She laughed, truly thrown by his answer. "Marrick killed his own sister? Why would he do that?"

"He didn't mean to. He lost control of his tiger and it killed her." He dropped his hands, freeing her.

"His tiger?" So there really was a tiger? But if so, why hadn't Craig and Marrick admitted it? Had Donna run into the animal? But the kids had said that their daddy had hurt their mommy.

"Marrick has a tiger?" She asked the question, but she wouldn't believe his answer.

"The kids think it was me because Donna and I had a fight, but it wasn't. It was Marrick who killed her."

"You're lying. You just said it was Marrick's tiger."

"I'm not lying."

"Then give me a reason why he'd kill his sister." Even if Marrick had a pet tiger and had lost control of it, she couldn't lay the blame squarely at his feet. Donna wouldn't have been out in the open, vulnerable, if she and John hadn't had a fight.

He's lying. The kids told the truth.

He had to be telling her a bullshit story to try and throw her off. Marrick with a tiger? It was impossible.

"They had an argument over their family's money. They've been fighting over their inheritance for years. He finally lost control of his tiger and it killed her."

She couldn't and wouldn't let him get away with such a ridiculous assertion. "Your story doesn't any sense. Besides, your kids said you hurt their mother."

He blinked, his expression going lax as though she'd caught him off guard. "They're mistaken. I don't blame them for saying it was me. They probably thought it was me, but it was Marrick. He must've had his back to them." He tugged on his black hair, hair so much like Marrick's.

"You just said it was his tiger." How dare he accuse Marrick. Her anger threatened to boil over. "You're a damn liar."

She expected him to get upset. Instead, he studied her, his eyes narrowing. "You don't know, do you?"

"Know what? Why don't you just spit it out? If what you're saying is true, then tell everyone your story." She didn't think a small town like Twisted would have a police force, maybe not even a sheriff, but they had to have some kind of law enforcement even if they had to call the authorities in a nearby town.

He scoffed. "It won't do me any good. Marrick's a big man around here. He's got everyone fooled into thinking he's a great guy. But me? Hell, I don't play their games and I tell them like it is whether they want to hear it or not. Some of those folks hate my guts because of the lies he's told them. They'll never believe me over him, especially with the kids mistaking him for me."

"Teag! Kitty!"

"Lisa!"

She started to turn around at the sound of the men's voices, but John clutched her arms again, keeping her facing him. "Listen to me if you want to stay safe. You can't trust Marrick or Craig."

"Lisa! Where the hell are you?" Craig's worried voice rang out.

She jerked free. "Over here!" When she turned back, John was gone.

"Lisa, what are you doing out here?"

She pivoted around to find Craig breaking through the brush and striding toward her. Suddenly, the fear she'd kept down came back, barreling into her. She fell into his arms, her hands fisting in his shirt.

"Hey, what's going on? Are you all right?" He pushed her back and skimmed his gaze along her body. "Are you hurt?"

"No, no. I'm okay. The kids took off running into the trees. Did you see them? We have to find them. I was chasing them when—"

"I found them." Marrick strode toward them with the kids in tow. "I swear they're getting faster every day." He stopped, his probing look fixed on her. "What's going on?"

Craig bent his head low, bringing her attention back to him. "Go on. You were chasing them when… When what, babe?"

What if John had told her the truth? Had she been duped into falling for Marrick and Craig? After all, she barely knew them.

"When I got lost." She buried her face against his chest, unable to look him straight in the eye and lie.

Craig wrapped his arms around her, giving her the comfort she needed, albeit for a different reason. Guilt hit her, but it wouldn't wipe away the worry plaguing her.

"Let's get these three back to the house," said Marrick.

She kept her gaze averted as Craig took her hand and started leading her home. What would she do now? Did she leave and never look back? She trusted Marrick and yet John had put doubts into her mind. If she left, would she be leaving the kids in the care of a murderer?

* * * *

Lisa was still trying to sort out her feelings when she carried the fish fillets and hot dogs outside to the backyard. Marrick was manning the grill, tossing lighter fluid on the coals. The flames leapt higher, increasing the crackling from the fire.

"There she is." Craig tossed the Frisbee to Teag who jumped up and snagged it out of the air. "We were wondering when you'd get out here."

"Sorry. I was busy trying to make sweet tea the way Lena does." She made an ugly face. "I failed big time and chucked it all down the sink."

"Don't worry about it. The kids can drink water. Craig and I are set." Marrick lifted a beer. "Do you want one?"

"No, thanks. I'll stick to water, too."

Kitty dashed in front of her, squealing her delight as she raced around the yard, chasing a butterfly. Her movements were graceful, her hair a shimmering dark stream flying behind her. She was the picture of happiness in her pretty sundress.

Not for the first time, Lisa wondered about the twins. She didn't know a lot about kids, but she couldn't help but think they were a lot more coordinated than other children their age. Even Teag's high flying jump into the air was more than she would've thought possible.

Not only did they have grace and coordination, they ran faster than the kids she liked to watch on the playground next to her apartment.

She handed the tray of fish and hot dogs off to Marrick. He made a "that looks yummy" face and set to work placing the food on the grill. The meat sizzled against the hot steel.

Lisa took a seat on the long bench of the picnic table where she could keep track of the children. Her heart soared as she watched them play. But her joy was short-lived as she shifted her gaze to Marrick and Craig standing side by side, their heads tilted toward each other.

Marrick couldn't have killed his sister. He was too nice a person to do such a horrible thing. Yet weren't a lot of murders considered "nice guys" by their neighbors and friends? Even by their loved ones?

Her attention went to Craig. If what John Bask had said was true, would Craig know? It was hard to believe Marrick would keep any secrets from his best friend, but it wasn't impossible.

She sighed, hating herself for having those ideas. She had to believe in them. If they weren't the men she thought they were, then she'd never trust another man again.

There was no way either man would be involved in Donna's death. Letting John talk her into believing such lies was just plain stupid.

Still... Why would John stick around if he wasn't telling the truth? If he'd killed his wife, why wasn't he halfway to Mexico by now?

"Don't worry, Marrick."

Craig's hand on his friend's shoulder brought her focus back to them.

"We're going to find that bastard and make him pay."

The men glanced her way, checking to see if she was listening. She averted her gaze then busied herself with pouring water out of the ice cold pitcher into her glass.

"Yeah, I know. I'm just pissed that it's taking so much time." Marrick speared a fish with a quick stab of his fork and flipped it over. "I would've thought he'd come after the kids by now."

"He knows the area as well as we do. There's a ton of places he could be hiding out. It takes time to check all of them." Craig took a swig of his beer. "Lena thinks we need to get the sheriff in on this. Or the state patrol."

"And let outsiders decide his fate?" Marrick's lip lifted into a snarl. "Not a chance. We deal with this our way. The tiger way."

The tiger way? Lisa inhaled sharply. Was John telling her the truth? Had Marrick somehow trained a white tiger to do as he commanded? To attack a person like a trained guard dog?

They looked her way again, this time catching her watching them.

"Is everything okay, baby?" asked Marrick. His dark gaze met hers, diving deep as though searching for the real answer.

She should've kept her mouth closed, but she was the type to put all her cards on the table. "You're going after John again? Why don't you turn the matter over to the authorities?" She would've sworn she saw a flash of amber in both Marrick's and Craig's eyes.

"Because that's the way it's done around here," answered Marrick. "We take care of our own."

"Are you talking about handling things like vigilantes?"

A muscle twitched in Craig's jaw. "We wouldn't call ourselves that, but we think our problems are better left to the people of Twisted. The outside world doesn't need to know our business." He grinned, obviously trying to ease the tension that had suddenly erupted between them. "What happens in Twisted, stays in Twisted."

She didn't smile, didn't laugh. Instead, she forced out the next question, hoping she'd get an answer that would calm her nerves. "And what will you do when you find him?"

Marrick turned his back to her. "We'll take care of him the way we've always taken care of those who do wrong."

It was harder to take a breath. "I'm afraid for you." *Of you.*

Craig strode toward her, moving faster than she'd have imagined any man could. In a moment, he was by her side, his fingers under her chin, making her raise her head to meet his gaze. "Are you afraid of us, babe?"

How had he known? Her body language must've clued him in. "Maybe. You're talking about killing a man, aren't you? Instead of taking him into custody and turning him over to the police? What about a trial? What about innocent until proven guilty?"

"He'll face the council." Craig slid his palm over her hair. "You've got to trust us on this. Twisted isn't like most places. We have our own way of doing things and it's worked well for a long time. John will get his say, but with the kids' testimony, his fate's pretty much sealed."

"What if the kids are wrong?"

Marrick turned back around. "Wrong? They saw their father."

She glanced at Teag and Kitty, making sure they were far enough away not to hear. The urge to tell the men about John was on the tip of her tongue, but something held her back. "I know, but they're young. Who knows what their imaginations might have done?"

"They saw what they said they saw." Marrick's expression turned cold. "You have to believe us. Kids around here are different. They grow up faster and their senses are a lot better than most."

He was right about that. Kitty and Teag had a way of picking up sounds she couldn't hear and sights she couldn't see. "Why is that, Marrick? I've noticed how fast they are and how much better their hearing and sight is."

He shrugged. "I guess children in Twisted are raised better. Maybe it's the clean living and the nutritious food they eat."

He was hiding the truth from her. What other truth was he keeping secret? "Oh, sure. Like hot dogs? Real good for them, huh?"

His smile could've melted any cold heart. She found herself wanting to believe him, needing to believe him. "Hey, the facts are the facts." He went back to tending the food.

"We're going to go out later." Craig took a seat next to her. "Are you okay staying with the kids? Would you like us to see if Lena can come out to keep you company?"

"I'm fine. Unless you think there might be a problem."

"Nah, no problem."

She looked down at the table, unwilling to let him see her eyes. "What if their father shows up?"

His arm snaked around her. "Then you give us a call. We know you'd do whatever you have to do to keep the kids safe."

"Yes, I would." But did that include getting them away from their uncle?

"Don't worry. We have a few of our friends watching the house, too."

She jerked her head up. "You have people watching the house while you're away? While I'm here?" She glanced around, suddenly feeling exposed and vulnerable. "Why didn't you tell me?"

He let out a sigh. "I guess we were afraid it might spook you into going home."

"You should've told me."

She didn't know whether to be angry or not. They'd done it to keep her and the children safe. Yet, it still felt like an invasion of her privacy. Then it hit her. Would they have friends watching the house if they didn't think John was a threat? The only reason to think so would be that he was indeed Donna's killer. Or was Marrick trying to keep the kids from their father so he couldn't convince them that they'd made a mistake? Her mind spun with the possibilities.

How do I know who to trust?

"Yeah, I know. You're right. We should have."

"When are your friends here? When are they watching?" Had they been around the day she'd run into John? If so, why hadn't they grabbed him?

"Just at night." Craig whispered in her ear. "There's another secret we need to tell you about."

That you have a pet tiger? A tiger trained to kill?

But she couldn't accuse them. Not until she knew more. Sometimes even those who liked to show their hand had to hold them against their chest. "What's the secret?"

He motioned to Teag and Kitty who were wrestling on the ground. Kitty could play as rough as her brother. "Be careful around Teag. He bites."

As if I don't already know.

As though on cue, Teag opened his mouth and bit down on his sister's hand. Kitty let out a wail and rolled away.

"Kitty!"

Craig caught her arm, keeping her in her seat. "Don't worry. He didn't bite hard enough to break the skin."

"But he shouldn't bite her at all."

"It's the way kids play around here." Marrick's previous stern expression was gone. "We let them work out their differences. See?"

He was right. Kitty held up her hands, her fingers extended like claws, and chased her brother around the yard. Both of the children were laughing and, as far as Lisa could see, Kitty wasn't bleeding.

"If you say so." After all, they knew their niece and nephew better than she did.

"Good." Marrick dug around in the coals with his fork and stabbed one of the foil wrapped potatoes. "Let's wrangle the kids and chow down."

Lisa nodded and poured water into two of the glasses while Craig shouted for Teag and Kitty to "get their butts over to the table." She paused, watching the children laugh as they dashed toward her.

Marrick and Craig were smiling, too, as they placed the food on the table. How could such great guys be bad? And yet, she'd gotten a glimpse of their anger and knew there was another side to them. What secret were they hiding?

Chapter Seven

Marrick was sore. Worse, he was angry. He and Craig had spent the night shifting back and forth between their human and tiger forms. Searching for John had become an obsession, one that was wearing him out. But he wouldn't rest until his sister's killer was found.

Would he turn John into the council as the others expected him to? Or would he exact his own vengeance? He'd had his mind made up until Lisa had started questioning him last night. She'd hated the idea of his giving John his due. That much was apparent. But her dislike of their plan wasn't what had churned in his gut all night.

She doesn't trust me.

Or, at least, she didn't act like she trusted him completely. Not like she had before. But what had changed her mind? His determination to do to John what the bastard had done to his sister?

She'd started giving him searching looks right after she'd gotten lost in the trees. How did anyone get lost anyway? She hadn't gone very far from the house.

No. Something else had to have happened. Something she wasn't telling him.

"We'll find him." Craig walked beside him.

From his friend's slow pace, he could see the all night search had taken its toll on him, too. "I know. But the longer it takes, the less chance we'll have of finding him."

"Maybe he lit out. We could contact the other prides to see if they've seen him. He has to show up somewhere."

White tigers were loners like most cats, but they also had a social side to them as well. Being a weretiger was rough enough even as part of a pride. As a lone cat, it would be even harder, leaving John exposed to the dangers of both hunters and other shifters.

"And when he does, someone will grab him," added Craig.

"I know John. He hasn't left. Not without his children." John Bask was an asshole with a temper that had taken its toll on Donna more than once. Yet he'd never known him to hurt his kids.

Craig slapped his arm against Marrick's chest. "Damn. What's that amazing smell?"

Marrick dragged in a long breath. The aroma was tantalizing, a welcome smell after a long, weary night. "Bacon and eggs. And coffee." He hurried up the deck and shoved through the door leading into the kitchen.

Lisa and the kids sat at the table covered with platters of food. A smile brightened her face as her gaze met his. "There you are. I was just about to go upstairs and wake you up." Her gaze slid over them. "I guess I didn't hear you go out."

She'd been fast asleep when they'd left late last night. Thankfully, she hadn't gotten up and found them gone.

Craig snared her, pulling her against him then planted a quick kiss on her cheek. "You, babe, are terrific. But did you really think we'd sleep this late?" He plopped into the chair next to Teag and took the platter of bacon away from the boy.

Even when they weren't out all night tracking down a killer, they would get up earlier than nine in the morning. Marrick came close to her, encouraged by her smile. He stopped a couple of feet away, once more sensing that she wasn't sure about him.

What had gone wrong between them? And more to the point, how did he fix it?

"Hey, baby, thanks for cooking all this." He spoke softly.

"No problem." She handed him a plate. "Here. Dig in."

"Don't mind if I do." He dared to slide his hand along her shoulders and was relieved when she didn't flinch. He took the chair closest to her then nodded his thanks when she picked up the coffee pot and filled his mug.

"A man could get used to this." Craig's words were muffled by the large bite he'd taken.

"Mommy said not to talk with your mouth full." Kitty arched an eyebrow at Craig.

"Your mom is right."

Kitty's eyes immediately filled with tears. Marrick could've kicked himself for not using the right tense. He should've said *was* and not *is*.

"Where's Daddy?" asked Teag.

Suddenly, the room was too quiet. No one wanted to answer his question. Yet it was his stoic sister who did. "Daddy hurt Mommy and he's never coming back. He said so."

Marrick dropped his fork to his plate. "When did he say he wasn't coming back?"

Kitty dropped her gaze. "I don't know."

He hated to force her to tell him, but he had to know. "Kitty, you have to tell me. When did you see your daddy?"

"I don't know."

Was she trying to keep from telling him or did she really not know? She was, after all, only five. Did children her age have a firm grasp on time?

"Was it the other day when you and Teag went into the trees by yourselves?" asked Lisa.

Marrick searched Lisa's face. Did she know something he didn't?

"Uh-huh."

He leaned toward his niece. "You saw your daddy? Did he talk to you?" His tiger clawed at the surface, angry at having been so close to its prey without realizing it.

"Uh-huh."

He had to be patient. If he tried to force answers from her, she'd clam up. He asked again, doing his best to keep his tone level. "Did you talk to your daddy, honey?"

"Uh-huh."

He clenched his hands under the table so she couldn't see them. "What did he say, Kitty? It's important that you tell me."

Kitty glanced at her brother, but Teag had his head down, trying hard not to get involved. "He said we could come with him when he was ready."

He'd been correct. John wasn't going anywhere without his kids. "What else did he say?"

She shook her head. "Nothing. He ran away again."

Marrick looked to Lisa. Had she scared him away? When he'd found the kids, he hadn't picked up on any clue that John had been there. Then again, he'd been focused on finding the kids and Lisa, not on picking up John's scent.

"Have you seen your daddy since then?"

"Marrick, maybe you shouldn't push." Lisa lifted her eyebrows in warning. "It might be too much."

But he couldn't let it go. Not if it helped him find their father. "Have you, Kitty?"

"Uh-uh." Her sorrowful big eyes met his. "I don't want to go with Daddy. He hurt Mommy."

"That's enough, Marrick." Lisa was on her feet and pulling the children into her arms. "Enough." She took them with her and left the kitchen.

"He was close. Real close," said Craig.

"And we missed him. Damn it." He sat back and struggled to keep from putting his fist through the table. "We missed him."

"It's okay, man. We'll get him the next time."

"Yeah, you're damn straight we will." John would come back and when he did, he'd be ready.

* * * *

Two more days had passed since the breakfast when Kitty had admitted to seeing her father. Many times, Lisa had started to tell Craig and Marrick that she, too, had seen him, but she just couldn't. Not until she was sure.

Yet how could she not be sure? Marrick, as well as Craig, had been wonderful to her. Other than when they were talking about John, she'd never see either one of the men angry. They were great with the children, too. As far as she was concerned, the way they treated Teag and Kitty showed their true character.

Then why couldn't she bring herself to tell them about seeing John? She trusted Marrick. She really did. And yet, a small part of her held back, fearful that her instincts were wrong. She'd agreed to stay on again, unwilling to leave until she knew for certain. But her doubt was also why she'd kept the men at a distance. If she were intimate with them again, she'd lose all chance of being objective.

"Lee-Lee! Ice cream! Ice cream!" shouted Teag.

He was off and running along the sidewalk toward the small treat shop before Lisa had a chance to stop him. "Teag, stop!" Kitty giggled and took off after him.

How can they run so fast?

Lisa ran, too, even though she had no chance of catching up. By the time she made it to the door of the shop, the kids were already inside, giving the teenage girl behind the counter their orders.

"You've got to be in shape to keep up with those two." Lena, who'd come up behind her, gave her a wink.

"Who says I'm keeping up with them?"

"Where are those luscious men of yours?"

Not for the first time, Lisa wondered if Lena was a cougar. She certainly liked younger men and yet she'd never seen her with any man, young or old.

"Back at the ranch. I promised the kids they could have an ice cream if they didn't quarrel today. And if Teag didn't bite his sister."

"Really? That's asking a lot of him." Lena wiggled her fingers at the kids. "Looks like he made it, though. They're really good kids. Too bad they've gone through such a tough time."

Without any warning, Lisa made a spur of the moment decision. "Can I ask you a question and get a straight answer?"

Surprise filled Lena's face. "Honey, if you don't know the answer to that question by now, then let me make it clear. I always tell the truth. Do I need to sit down before you ask?"

"Maybe."

Lena's eyes widened. "Really bad, huh? Go ahead. Ask me."

She swallowed, suddenly sure she'd made a mistake. And yet, she couldn't hold back any longer. "Did Marrick and his sister fight over their inheritance?"

"Honey, you're throwing me for a loop. What inheritance? Do you mean the money their parents left them?"

"Right. Did they fight about it?"

"Not at all. From what I heard, there wasn't much money to start with. As the son, Marrick inherited the ranch from his father like most men around here do."

"So Donna didn't get anything?" Had Donna wanted more? Wasn't money often a motive for murder?

"Donna didn't want the ranch. By the time their parents passed— their mother going first and then their father a few months later—she was already married to John. Instead, she asked Marrick to pay her a third of what the ranch was worth."

"And did he?" A knot formed in her stomach.

"No, he didn't."

Oh, no. Was it true? Had John told her the truth?

"He paid her half what it was worth. Said it was only fair. Then when Craig came down to help him run the place, he sold half of it to him." Lena narrowed her eyes. "Why do you ask?"

"I was just wondering, is all." She was so relieved, she wanted to hug the woman. "I'd better get inside before the kids eat everything in sight."

Before she could, Lena caught her by the arm. "Where are all these questions coming from?"

"Like I said. Just curious." She felt horrible. After asking Lena to tell her the truth, she was lying to her. At least by omission.

"I have a feeling you're not being open with me."

"I really need to get inside with the kids. Talk to you soon, Lena."

Plastering on a wide smile, she hurried into the shop. Teag and Kitty were seated at a small table. The boy had chocolate surrounding his mouth and dribbled down the front of his shirt. Kitty was busy catching the drips off her cone.

"Hey, you two, no more running off. Am I understood?"

They both nodded, too engrossed in their treats to bother speaking.

"Would you like a cone, ma'am?"

Ma'am. Argh. I feel so old.

She shook her head at the young girl. "No thanks. What do I owe you for theirs?"

"Nothing. It's on the house." The girl's gaze slid to the kids as her smile faded. "You know. Because."

Because they lost their mother. Because their father was a murderer.

Lisa sat down next to Teag who had devoured his ice cream. She took a napkin and wiped his face clean. "Wow, you sure finished yours fast."

Kitty held her cone out to her, offering her a lick. "Want some?"

"Okay. Thanks." She supported Kitty's hand and took a lick. The ice cream tasted more like straight cream to her, richer than regular ice cream, but it was still good. "Yum."

Kitty giggled and caught another drip. "Yum."

An older gentleman sat at the next table reading the paper. He lowered it and scowled. "Can't you keep those kids quiet? I don't want to hear them yammering away."

Teag bared his teeth then made a chomping action. "I'll bite you."

"The hell you will, boy. Teach those kids some manners." The old man's glower deepened. "And shut them the hell up."

"They've barely said anything." She didn't want to be rude, but sometimes it was impossible not to speak up. "If you wanted peace and quiet, maybe you should've gone somewhere besides a treat shop. You know. Where there might not be any kids?"

"Look, girl, don't go giving me any sass." He plopped the paper on the table. "You need to respect your elders."

"I do respect those elders who deserve respect." Why was she letting him get to her? Maybe the stress of the past few days, worrying if what John had said was true, had gotten to her. She drew in a long, slow breath. "I'm sorry, sir. We'll do our best to keep the noise down."

Kitty giggled. "Mommy says his hiss is worse than his scratch."

Teag laughed and joined in. "Uh-huh. Daddy said he's a big old pussy cat who's too old to have claws."

Lisa laughed, more at the way Teag had said it than at what he'd said. Kids said crazy things, even things that didn't always make sense.

At the sound of a low grumble, she turned toward the man, ready to apologize for her laughter and their remarks. Her mouth was open ready to speak before she stopped and stared at him.

Amber filled the old man's eyes. His mouth drew back into a snarl exposing non-human teeth. Fangs dripped saliva, the droplets falling onto his shirt. She followed one drip as it landed on his hand. Claws had replaced fingernails.

Lisa pushed to her feet, shoving the chair out from under her while clutching an arm of each child. "Run," she whispered.

Kitty dropped her cone and let out a wail. "Noooo! My ice cream!"

Teag struggled to get loose. "Hey!"

Adrenaline surged through Lisa as she pulled the children along with her. At the door, she glanced back over her shoulder, fearful the man was following them. His amber gaze struck her, numbing her for a moment. Then, spreading his jaws wide, he let out a vicious snarl.

"Oh, shit." She shoved the children outside, still clinging to them.

Was he coming after them? She hadn't noticed where the teen had gone. Should she yell for help? And yet, the street had suddenly emptied.

She hurried away from the shop. Where could they go? Where would they find at least one person to help them?

Roar.

There was always someone at the bar.

Looking back again, she saw the man push open the door and stumble after her. Thankfully, he seemed too old to move very fast. Darkness covered his face along his jawlines as though he'd suddenly grown a beard. Squinting, she realized it wasn't hair.

It's fur. Oh, hell, he's growing fur.

Racing across the street, she ignored the children's complaints and made it to the bar's door. Whether or not children were allowed inside didn't matter. She had to get help before the monster-man caught them.

Bursting inside Roar, she let her eyes adjust to the dim light. Although it was late afternoon, only a few people were seated at the tables.

"Lisa, what's wrong? You act like you've seen a ghost."

She pivoted around to see a man she'd met a few days ago slide off a bar stool and stride toward her. "Marvin, please. You've got to help us."

"What's wrong?" Marvin Robbins was around Marrick's and Craig's age and worked as a hired hand for all the ranchers.

"This man…" How could she explain it without sounding insane? "This man in the treat shop got angry. Then he started changing." She still clung to Teag and Kitty. "He's chasing us."

The door banged opened. Daylight slashed into the bar. The shadow of the old man blocked out some of the light. A growl rolled out of the dark shadow as he took a step forward.

She gasped. What had been a human face was now a strange contortion of animal and man. Dark gray fur spread over most of his face, highlighting the amber eyes. He was breathing hard as his body grew fuzzy. She rubbed her eyes, but it didn't help. It wasn't her eyesight causing the blurred vision. The man was changing. But changing into what?

"Marvin?" Lisa hurried to the wall, putting her body between the terrible man and the kids. "Oh, God."

"Damn it, Herb. What the hell do you think you're doing?" Purdy stormed out from behind the bar. "Marrick and Craig haven't told her yet."

Stunned, Lisa looked at the others in the bar. No one, including Marvin, were afraid of the beast-man. "They haven't told me what yet?"

Marvin and Purdy exchanged a telling glance as Marvin came toward her. She shook her head, all at once afraid to have any of them near her. Was she losing her mind? Didn't they see what she saw?

"Lisa, I'm sure the guys didn't want you to find out like this. Damn it, Herb." Marvin's lip lifted into a snarl.

"Tell me what? That there's a monster in your town?" Her thoughts whirled, bringing up one idea only to lose it. Was John a beast-man? Was that why they couldn't get the authorities involved in finding him?

"Monsters? Hell, Lisa, watch who you're calling monsters." Another man she'd seen before, a man who had been kind to her, scowled. He'd been leaning back in his chair then dropped it down, planting his feet.

"Haskel?"

"Yeah. That's right. I met you the other day at the market." He started to come toward her, but Marvin blocked his way. "Come on, guys. The cat's out of the bag now. She's got to find out sooner or later. Looks like old Herb here decided on sooner."

"Marvin, please. What's going on?"

Marvin's expression said it all. He knew exactly what was happening. "Lisa, I know this will be hard to understand…" He paused. "Then again, now that you've seen Herb, maybe it won't be."

She tried to breathe, tried to calm herself. But how could she? The world had been turned upside down.

"I'm just gonna say it plain out." Marvin swept his arm around the room. "We're shape-shifters. People who can change into animals."

Herb's growl interrupted Marvin. "Purdy, get hold of Herb. He never did have good control over his tiger."

Purdy moved to do what Marvin had asked, but Herb let out another growl. Suddenly, his clothes started tearing away. Fur burst through the seams and clawed feet broke out of his boots.

Lisa clapped a hand over her mouth as the man changed, going from human into a large white tiger.

I really did see a tiger.

Amazingly, Purdy grabbed hold of the tiger's tail and started pulling him toward the back room.

She let out a small moan. "Oh, my God." Marvin reached for her, but she backed away.

"Try to calm down, Lisa. No one's going to hurt you."

She scanned the bar. Every set of eyes were on her. Some of those eyes were glowing with bits of amber. "You're all the same?"

Marvin nodded. "Yes, but you don't need to be afraid. We won't hurt you."

I have to get out of here. I have to keep the kids safe.

Taking hold of their hands, she darted past Marvin and out the door.

"Lisa! Hold up. We won't hurt you!" called Marvin.

"Honey, what's going on?"

She skirted past Lena, hurrying as fast as she could and still hang onto the kids. They made it to Marrick's pickup and she slung the door opened.

"Get inside. Fast."

"Lisa, honey, don't go. Let us explain."

She stared at Lena. Her, too?

There was no way in hell she was going to stick around. Hopping into the truck, she turned the key and slammed on the gas. By the time she dared to glance in the rearview mirror, Lena and Marvin were standing in the middle of the street, watching.

Chapter Eight

"I'm going to kill that fucking Herb." Craig didn't know if Marrick could hear him or not over the thundering sound of their horses' hooves digging into the dry Texas ground. He didn't care. He'd said it as much for himself as for his friend.

Lena's call had them hightailing it back to the ranch. He just hoped they'd get there before Lisa did. According to Lena, Lisa wasn't about to hang around. She'd no doubt hot-foot it out of town. Since the twins were with her, she'd probably take them along for safe keeping.

He could see the pickup she'd borrowed parked in front of the house in a haphazard way, half on the grass and half on the cement parking pad. If she'd taken her car into town, she might not have come back to the ranch. Thankfully, her car had started acting up the day before.

Marrick brought his horse to a skidding stop along with his. Together, they were off their mounts and bounding up the front steps when she burst through the door.

"Oh, thank God you're back." Lisa clutched the front of Craig's shirt. "You're never going to believe what I found out. The tiger I saw? It's real and they're more of them."

"Calm down, babe."

She shook her head causing her curls to dance. "No, I can't. Don't you see? They know I know about them now. They'll be coming after us. We have to get out of here while we can. Please, let's go."

He looked to Marrick for an answer, but his friend gave him a slight shake, his mouth set in a thin line. Craig took hold of her arms.

Should he slap her? Did that really help when someone was hysterical or did it only make them even more upset?

"Where are the kids?"

"They're inside. I told them to put some clothes and toys into garbage bags. I didn't know if they had suitcases."

"Okay." Craig hooked his arm in hers as much to try and comfort her as to lead her back inside. Once in the living room, he called to the kids. "Teag. Kitty. Are you two all right?"

"Uh-huh," called Kitty.

At least they were within shouting distance. "Stay where you are until we call you, okay?"

"Okay," answered Teag.

"No. We need to leave. Now." She yanked her arm out of his. "You don't understand. There are monsters in Twisted. They can change into big white tigers."

"Babe—"

"No, Craig, it's true. I saw one of them change." Her eyes were wild, her breaths lifting her chest in rapid succession. "Marvin, Haskel, even Purdy. They all said it was true. They're monsters, too."

Monsters? He never would've believed she'd think of them as monsters. She'd be shocked, sure, but monsters were horrible creatures that harmed people.

Craig cringed when Marrick took hold of her and gave her a quick shake. "Lisa, knock it off. You're not in any danger." Bits of amber blazed in his eyes. "Not from them and not from us, either."

She frowned, confusion marring her forehead. When she tilted her head to the side much like weretigers did, Craig knew she finally understood. Her mouth opened into a small *oh*.

Where she'd been afraid before, now she was in full panic mode. "No. It can't be. You can't be."

Now that Marrick had told her, there was no turning back. "Babe, try and understand. We won't hurt you. Not now. Not ever."

"You're like them? You're shape-shifters?" She moved backward until her legs hit the couch. "I thought it was crazy to think you owned one, but that you *are* one? No. I won't. I can't."

Where had she gotten the idea that they owned a tiger?

"Yes, but, babe, we're still us. Nothing you know about us is any different."

"Except that you can change into animals. Are you white tigers, too?" She sat down hard. "Nooo. This isn't real. I must be dreaming. Or hurt. Unconscious."

Craig shoved the coffee table out of the way and went to his knees. He reached out for her, but she let out a small yelp and jerked away from him. "Lisa, please, don't be afraid. We're still the same guys. Try to calm down."

She shook her head, intent on denying the truth. "I can't. I saw him change. He was huge. And, oh, God, the fangs." Her gaze dropped to his hands. "And his claws. No, please, tell me it's all a bad dream."

Marrick flattened his hands on the arm chair and bent forward. "Damn it, Lisa, stop acting like an idiot. This is real. *We* are real. Just deal with it."

Craig couldn't hold back the growl that slipped from his lips. "Fuck off, man. You're not helping."

"She has to accept the truth. She's our mate. What else can she do?" Marrick reared back and dragged a hand through his hair.

"Your mate?"

Craig wasn't sure if she was beginning to calm down or if she was so freaked out she couldn't move. "Can you listen to us, babe? I mean, really listen?"

She drew in a shaky breath. "I'll try."

It was more than he'd dared to hope for. "Good." He came to sit beside her, thankful when she allowed him to take her hands in his. "It's true. We're weretigers. Shape-shifters. Men who can change into tigers."

She closed her eyes, shuddered, and then opened them again. Tears welled in them.

"Remember. We'd never hurt you. Not for any reason." She needed to hear him promise her safety several times. Each time he did, he noticed a small flash of relief on her face. "Shape-shifters have been around forever just like humans. We don't attack people. All we want to do is to live in peace without the world finding out about us. Can you understand what I'm saying?"

"Y–yes."

"Then please understand the rest. As weretigers, we know that one day we'll find the woman we'll love for the rest of our lives. She's our intended mate."

He could see her trying to grasp what he was saying. She struggled with it, but at least she tried.

"And I'm your mate?"

"Right." He smiled, trying again to comfort her.

Marrick had finally calmed down. He sat in the arm chair and rested his elbows on his knees. "I'm sorry I yelled at you. It's just with the kids and Donna—" He paused, gathering himself. "I'm sorry."

She nodded, forgiving Marrick. Things were starting to look a little better. Maybe.

"Do you feel something every time you're with us? Remember? We talked about it before. Something more than just that we're so incredibly hot?" *A joke couldn't hurt, right?*

His reward was a slight lift of the corners of her mouth. "Yes. It's like an electric current. Or a really strong rope pulling me toward you."

"Have you ever felt anything like it before?"

"No. Nothing."

"That's what we call the connection. It's what brings mates together."

"Like fate?"

"Exactly," answered Marrick. "We don't believe it's a coincidence that you came to Twisted." His expression darkened. "We only wish you hadn't had to go through what you have. Finding Donna's body and hearing about what we are from someone else. I know it's been rough on you."

Her sorrowful expression mirrored Marrick's. Craig didn't want anything to sideline the real discussion. "But meeting you is fate. It's the connection at work. You're our intended mate and you came. If you'll accept us as your mates, as your partners in life, then we'll do our dead level best to make you happy."

"I'm your mate? Like being married? To the both of you?"

At least she'd started breathing easier. "That's right. We can't both legally marry you, but it's the same thing."

"I can't believe this. It's all too much."

"You're going to need time to let it sink in." Marrick put his hand on her leg. Surprisingly, she didn't jump at his touch. "We'll give you all the time you need, but you've got to promise you won't leave. If you do—"

"If you do, it'll break our hearts," interrupted Craig. "Weretigers only have one mate. If you turn us down, we'll live out our lives missing you."

"You said you felt the connection, right?" asked Marrick.

She glanced at the both of them. "Yes. If that's what it's called. Yes."

"Then will you stay? I swear no one will hurt you." Craig's heart was in his throat. If she still wanted to leave, they wouldn't stop her.

"You can change into tigers. I still can't believe it."

Was it a question? Or was she trying to convince herself? "Yes. Marrick and I are weretigers."

Her eyes grew big again. "And the twins? Are they—?"

"Yes. Donna was human, but John was a weretiger. The kids were born weretigers." He didn't want to talk about anyone but them. She had to adjust to what they were first before trying to accept anyone else.

"Oh, hell. No wonder they're so damn fast."

He chuckled at her amazement. "Yeah. And they have sensitive hearing and their other senses are heightened, too."

"Can they change?"

"Not yet. Once they get into puberty, though, then watch out." Having one teenage weretiger would be hard enough, but two? He and Marrick would need all the help they could get.

"Wow." She fell back, slumping in her seat. "Do they know what you are? What they are?"

"After today, they definitely know about shifters. Hell, judging from the way they didn't freak out, they've probably known for a while. Some kids find out early on after seeing a relative or friend shift. I'm not sure what Donna told them." He looked to Marrick for an answer, but got none. "We could ask to be sure, but then we'd have to tell them about us."

"I want to see what you look like."

He'd expected as much. Wanting to see, needing to confirm with her own eyes what she'd been told wasn't unusual. Even though she'd seen Herb change at Roar, she still needed to see them in their tiger bodies.

"Let me check on the kids and tell them to stay in their room first. Go on and start without me if you want." Marrick bounded up the stairs and headed down the hallway.

"Are you sure, babe? I wouldn't want you to be afraid."

"I'm sure." She clasped her hands in her lap, her knuckles turning white.

"Okay. I'm going to get undressed first." He stood and started unbuttoning his shirt.

"So you won't tear your clothes, right?"

"Right. I guess Herb didn't bother changing before he shifted?"

She drew in a long steadying breath. "No. He got so angry so fast, I don't think he gave it any thought. He came after us when we ran out of the sweet shop."

"He's a cranky old fart and flies off the handle a lot. I'm sorry you had to find out about us that way."

She didn't respond. Instead, her gaze fixed on him as he slowly took off his clothes.

Damn it. Don't get turned on.

Yet having her watch him was doing exactly that. "Babe, uh, I don't usually have a hard on when I shift. It's just that you're watching so…"

Another smile earned. He could spend the rest of his life earning her smiles.

"I'm just saying, is all." He let his shirt drop to the floor. Her gaze locked on to his chest. Was he strong enough for her? Broad enough? If not, he'd buy a home gym and work out every day.

"You're taking it kind of slow, aren't you? We'll have to make this quick because of the kids." Marrick strode into the room. His shirt was gone and he had his boots off and was working on the zipper of his jeans.

The bulge of his crotch said Marrick was having the same problem he was.

"The kids are busy watching a movie they like. They should be good for another hour or so. I made sure they understood to stay in their room." Marrick kicked off his jeans.

Craig was almost jealous when she slipped her attention to his friend. Almost. They'd decided to share a woman early on. Besides, he liked watching her with Marrick. He toed off his boots then shoved his jeans down.

The tip of her tongue slipped between her lips.

No doubt about it. She's as turned on as we are.

But first things first. She had to accept them for what they were.

"Are you sure you're ready?" The last thing they needed was to frighten her again.

"Yes. Please. I have to see this."

"Okay." He glanced at Marrick. "Let's do this."

Together, they turned their inner tigers free. The transformation came quickly as years of changing had taught him. Bones broke and fur spread over his body. Amber colored the world around him as he watched Lisa sit up and grip the edge of the couch.

Please, don't run.

If she did, he'd have to chase her. First in his tiger body, and then changing once he caught her.

His breathing picked up speed as it always did, yet he knew part of it was due to his nerves. Would she run? Would she accept them? Would she see what they were and decide she couldn't handle a life with shape-shifters?

Even as his cat mind took over, the thoughts continued to pummel him. As a man ideas were concrete things. As a tiger, they were more like feelings, lacking clear substance and order. As the change continued, he dropped onto his hands and knees as claws replaced fingers.

"Oh, hell."

He might not have heard her if his weretiger hearing hadn't caught her whisper.

Please, don't run.

* * * *

What Lisa saw was unbelievable. Even after seeing it once before, seeing the men she cared for change into tigers still made her heart pound and her mind whirl, trying to deny what her eyes showed her.

They really are white tigers.

Within minutes, Marrick and Craig no longer existed. In their places were two amazing, deadly creatures that could kill her with one quick swipe of their paws. Their glowing amber gazes fixed on her, keeping her glued to the couch.

If I ran, would they chase me?

The logical side of her screamed at her to flee. To get away from the house and Twisted as fast as she could.

Yet the strange sensation drawing her to them every time they came near her was still there. She wasn't turned on in a sexual way, but found she still needed them. She still wanted them at her side, day and night, for as long as she lived.

The connection. That's what they'd called it. It was a simple name for an extraordinary sensation. And yet it fit.

Craig eased closer then set his large head on her knee. At first, she jerked back, but then an overwhelming sense of peace permeated her. He'd never hurt her. She knew that as well as she knew her own name. His soft purr sent a flow of warm air over her knee.

"Craig."

A low growl had her whipping her hand back. Marrick, looking all the world like he was jealous, gave another growl and placed his head on her other knee. Were they competing for her attention?

Tentatively, she put a palm on each of their broad heads. Their fur was as soft as she'd thought it would be. The warmth from their bodies radiated through her hand along with the sizzle of the connection. They were huge, dwarfing her in size.

"You're beautiful. Amazing."

Their black stripes were perfectly placed along their bodies. Whiskers tickled her arms and their purrs calmed her nerves. Their tails swished from one side to the other. Like two well-trained dogs, they sat down on their haunches and gazed up at her, ready to follow her commands.

"No one's ever going to believe me."

Slowly, carefully, she went to her knees, positioning her body between them. Her arms slipped around their necks as she pulled them close. "You feel so good."

What would it be like to be one of them? Would she be able to change if she accepted them as her mates?

Their purrs grew louder until, at last, the one who was Marrick pulled back. He padded a few feet away. Craig nuzzled his nose against her neck, made a soft mewing sound, and then eased away to stand next to his friend.

"You're changing back, aren't you?"

She blinked, their bodies blurring again as the transformation began. Would she get used to the awful sound of their bones breaking? Did it hurt? Were they hiding the pain from her?

A few minutes later, the men were back in their human bodies.

Craig pulled on his jeans and tugged on his shirt. "Are you okay, babe?"

"You're men again." She sounded like an idiot, stating the obvious, yet somehow it helped.

Marrick glanced toward the ceiling. "If the kids weren't here, I'd show you just how much of a man I am."

Oh, how she longed for him to do exactly that with Craig joining in. "I still can't believe what I saw."

Craig retook his place next to her. "Like Marrick said, it's going to take time."

"The main thing to remember is that you can trust us to take care of you." Marrick joined them on the couch then glanced at Craig as though seeking silent permission. "We love you, Lisa. Both as men and as tigers."

"The real questions are these." Craig's gray eyes studied her. "Do you love us? Can you accept what we are? Do you want us as your mates? Do you want to live with us and be our woman for the rest of your life?"

Could she? Was a life with them what she wanted?

The uncertainty about Marrick still remained. And yet, every time she looked at him, she knew John Bask had to be lying. Craig and

Marrick were good men. Men she could trust no matter what anyone else said.

"What do you say, baby?" Marrick leaned forward and grazed the back of his fingers over her cheek. "Want to be ours?"

"Lisa, we're hungry."

Lisa twisted around at the sound of Kitty's voice. The twins pounded down the stairs and into the living room. If they'd come in a minute earlier, they would've seen everything.

She needed time to think, time to sort out her feelings. The children had bought her that time. "I'll stay. For now. But I'm going to need time."

"Lisa—"

"No, Marrick. We said we'd give her the time she needs." Craig stood taking her along with him. "But you're staying for now, right? You won't leave?"

"I won't leave. At least not before I give you my answer." She eased past Marrick toward the kids. "Who wants a peanut butter and jelly sandwich?"

Lisa followed the kids into the kitchen area, leaving the men in the living room. "Kitty, please get the jelly out of the fridge. Teag, you can get the big jar of peanut butter out of the pantry."

"Really?" Teag stared at her with eyes so much like his sister's.

"Yes. Really." She didn't blame him for being surprised. She'd had to order him to stay out of the pantry. The last time he got into the closet-like space, he'd made a huge mess. But right then, she wasn't sure she could hold anything with her hands shaking so hard.

She'd bought some time to think. But how long did it take for a person to come to grips with the impossible?

Chapter Nine

They're watching me again.

Lisa should've minded, but she didn't. Craig and Marrick were obviously anxious to get her answer.

They'd said they loved her. Since the moment they'd told her, a firestorm of emotions had erupted, bringing forth questions she hadn't dared to ask herself.

Did she love them?

The answer surprised her, coming back fast and furious.

I do love them.

How the hell did that happen?

"Read us a story," demanded Teag. He kicked the covers she had lovingly tucked around him, messing up the bed. "Read us a story or I'll bite you."

Lisa gave him a stern look. He'd given her the same threat earlier and she'd called his bluff. Unfortunately, he hadn't been bluffing. But at least he hadn't bitten down hard enough to break the skin.

"I might if you remember how to ask nicely. And no more biting, young man." He was a stubborn child who had to be told multiple times before he'd listen. Still, she had to hold back a grin. He was stubborn, yes, but he was so damn cute.

Kitty snuggled into her covers. "Pulease, Lee-Lee?"

"See, Teag?" Lisa bopped him lightly on the nose. "That's how you ask nicely."

He pushed out his lower lip as his stubborn streak fought with his yearning to hear a story. Finally, he gave in. "Pulease, Lee-Lee?"

"I'd love to. So which book will it be?" She held up three of their favorite books.

"All of them!" shouted Teag.

Lisa tilted her head and arched an eyebrow. It didn't take long for Kitty to catch on.

"*The Big Bad Werewolf.*" Kitty held up her hands and formed claws then growled.

Did werewolves exist, too? She'd have to ask the men.

"*The Big Bad Werewolf* it is." Opening the book, she waited until the twins settled down, and then started reading. Yet although she read aloud, her mind wandered.

What am I going to do?

Thirty minutes later, after reading two more books, she looked up from the last page and saw the children's eyes closed, their chests rising and falling as they breathed in through their opened mouths. Returning the books to the shelf, she left the room as quietly as she could.

Craig and Marrick were in the living room, waiting for her as she'd known they would be. They were stretched out, reminding her of two lazy cats, their eyes half-closed and their bodies relaxed as though they were boneless.

"Are they asleep?" asked Marrick, his tone eager.

"Sure are." She moved to the couch, settling in between them. "I need to ask you some questions. Hey, wait a minute. Aren't you two going out looking for John Bask?"

"We decided we needed to be with you tonight." Craig caressed her arm then leaned in for a kiss. The kiss, however, ended all too soon.

Were they afraid to leave her alone? Did they think she'd take off?

"Go ahead. Ask away." Marrick was suddenly nervous, his body going tense.

She took a deep breath to steady her own nerves. "First of all, I need to tell you what happened the other day in the trees."

"The day you got lost?"

Saying she was lost was a lame excuse and she didn't blame Craig for the question in his tone. She leaned closer, letting the tingle of desire rush between them. The connection was stronger than ever.

I might as well get it out.

"I saw John Bask."

Both men came to attention, leaning even closer.

"What? Why the fuck didn't you say anything?" Marrick stared at her as though she'd lost her mind.

"Hang on, Marrick. Babe, did he hurt you?" Craig seemed more worried than angry.

"No, he didn't do anything to me and I don't know why I didn't call out." She cringed, knowing she'd just lied. If she was going to make a life with the men, she had to tell them everything. "I'm sorry. That's not true. I didn't call for you because at first I was so surprised to see him that I didn't think. Then he told me about Marrick."

Marrick couldn't have looked any more shell-shocked if she'd asked him to hold a grenade. "About me? What'd he say?"

She hated like hell to tell them, hated that she'd ever believed John. Hoping they'd forgive her for keeping quiet, she blurted out the truth. "He said you and Donna had an ongoing argument about the inheritance your folks left you. He said you cheated your sister out of her share."

She couldn't look at Marrick to see his reaction. She didn't have to. The fury oozed out of him.

"That bastard," muttered Craig. "You know he's lying, right?

"I do now, but at the time, I wasn't sure about a lot of things." She gathered her resolve, determined to hold nothing back. "But that's not the worst of it."

"Go on. What did the asshole say?" Craig had grown angrier by the second.

"He told me you and Donna got into a fight." She forced her gaze to meet Marrick's. "He said you're the one who killed her."

Marrick's mouth fell open. He sat back, staring even harder at her.

"That son of a bitch." Craig bolted up and paced to the other side of the room. "I swear, once we find him, I'm going to tear his lying tongue out."

Marrick, however, remained silent.

"Marrick? Are you all right?"

His jaw worked, tensing and releasing the muscle there. "And you believed him."

If only she could've been anywhere else at the moment. Yet she'd already waited too long to tell him. "I was scared and he was so convincing."

"You've got to be kidding. You believed him?" Craig shot her an accusatory glare.

"Maybe. For a while. But I don't think I ever really thought it was true. If I had, I would've left." Had she thrown everything they might have together out the window? Had one stupid mistake ruined it all?

Marrick got up, making her ache to reach out, grab his arm, and keep him by her side. He went to the other side of the room. "What do you believe now, Lisa?"

Was he willing to listen? Was he willing to forgive her?

"I know who you are, Marrick. I've watched you with the twins and I've seen how you are with other people. And how you treat me. There's no way in hell you could've hurt your sister."

"Are you sure?" His anger was gone, replaced by sadness.

Seeing him hurting was worse than seeing him angry. "Yes. I'm sure." She had to get all her feelings out. "Part of why it was so hard was because I could sense you were holding something back. Now I know you were. I don't blame you, but it didn't help to know you weren't being completely honest with me."

"We couldn't tell you. You would've run off. As it was, if it weren't for the kids, we're not sure you would've stayed even with the connection between us. I guess we were as confused as you were." Craig came back to the couch, his body relaxing as the anger left him.

"I sensed you were keeping a secret, that you knew more than you were letting on." She glanced from one man to the other. "And you were."

"She's got us there," admitted Craig.

"Then there was this strange, exhilarating sensation whipping between us. I didn't know what to think, yet I was sure you weren't telling me everything. About John Bask and more."

"She's right. We can't blame her for letting John get to her. Not when we weren't coming clean with her." Craig twisted toward his friend. "What are you thinking?"

Reading Marrick was hard to do. His expression had gone neutral.

"Marrick? Can you forgive me for thinking you could ever hurt your sister?"

"We lied to her." Craig's tone implored his friend. "By my way of thinking, we're in the wrong more than she is."

"If you'd called for us, we could've caught him." Marrick's anger was back. "This nightmare would be over."

"You're right. I should have."

"Come on, man. Give her a break. You know how convincing John can be. He can talk a mole out of a hole when he wants to."

Marrick stared out the front window, putting his back to her. If Craig hadn't taken her hand to comfort her, she wasn't sure she could've stayed in her seat and waited.

"I'm sorry, Marrick. I really am."

He whirled around and stalked over to her. For a moment, he stood there, towering over her. Then, suddenly, he dropped his hands to the back of the couch, capturing her between his arms.

Lust swallowed her whole. Every fiber of her being wanted nothing more than to be with them. She squeezed Craig's hand as she searched Marrick's face. If he threw her out, she'd never be able to get over them.

"Do you trust us? Really trust us?"

She'd half expected Marrick to yell at her and demand she leave. Instead, he'd asked one of the questions she'd wrestled with since seeing John. Her decision had been made hours before, making answering him easy.

"Yes. I trust you." Only a weretiger could've heard her almost inaudible response.

"Do you love us?"

Surprised, she held back even though the answer was already on the tip of her tongue. Meeting his gaze dead-on, she gave him the one and only truth that really mattered. "Yes. I love you. Both of you."

"Good. Then no more doubting us. Got it?"

"Yes."

"And you're staying. Not for the kids, but for us. Right?"

"Yes. But I love them, too."

"Good enough."

She let out a small yelp of surprise as Marrick took her under the arms and yanked her upward. He was already taking the stairs before she realized she was slung over his hard shoulder.

Craig chuckled as he followed behind them. Marrick stalked toward her bedroom.

She couldn't contain her joy, laughing as she playfully beat on his back, pretending to want to be set free. It seemed like forever since their time in the barn. She'd hungered for them since that day, but until her body had touched Marrick's, she hadn't realized just how much she'd thirsted for them.

She was still laughing when he tossed her on top of the bed.

"Be quiet. We don't want to wake up the kids," warned Craig.

She nodded, but her attention wasn't on what he said. Her passion flared to a higher level as Craig unbuttoned his shirt. Every inch he exposed turned her on more. Every hair on his chest was a signal to her pussy to get ready. She dug her fingernails into the covers, doing her best to resist jumping up and tearing his shirt away.

Hurry, damn it.

Her gaze shifted to Marrick. *Now that's the way to do it.*

Marrick's shirt was already open. He'd torn it apart, letting buttons scatter everywhere. His chest was as amazing as his friend's with as many hard ridges topped with stone-like pecs. Six packs weren't the way they were built. Their abdomens were eight packs of warm flesh she ached to skim her fingers over.

Craig's shirt was finally off. He and Marrick started working on the button on the jeans, and then the zipper. She swallowed, already imagining the taste of their cocks, the texture of their skin as she ran her tongue over their lean bodies.

Their wide shoulders led to rounded arms of toned muscles. Strong arms came to strong hands. The V's of the stomachs led the way downward to the treasures that waited underneath the simple denim. Their jeans hung on their hips until she was forced to take her eyes up to their faces. What were they waiting for?

"Guys?" She sat up, praying they hadn't changed their minds.

"Strip, baby," ordered Marrick.

Suddenly, she was shy. It didn't make any sense. They'd already seen her naked. They knew what her body looked like. And yet, having them stand there, watching, made her nervous.

"Go on. We want to see your beautiful body."

She warmed, thrilled by Craig's praise. Slowly, she tugged the shirt over her head and wished she'd put on a prettier bra and panties. Not that it would matter. They wouldn't keep them on her very long.

Two low growls of pleasure rumbled and their eyes sparked with amber. She pushed the hair out of her face. "Just to be sure, you don't change while having sex, do you?"

"I won't lie." Craig heeled off his boots, reaching down to tug one off, making his back and arm muscles ripple with the effort. "Our tigers rise to the surface when we get turned on, but we'd never turn them loose."

"Unless you wanted us to," added Marrick. "If you decide you want us to change you into a weretiger, then tiger sex can be a lot of fun. Rough, but fun."

"You can do that? Change me into one of you?" Would she want to be a weretiger? The idea was fascinating, yet scary.

"If you want. It's up to you."

"What about having kids?" She hoped the subject wouldn't diminish their lust for her. Yet, instead, the glint in their eyes said differently.

"We want kids. Do you?" Marrick dropped his jeans, letting his erect cock jump outward and point straight at her.

For a moment, she forgot what the question was. "I'm sorry? What'd you say?" His cock was magnificent. Long, curved with dark veins running the length of it. Pre-cum glistened on the end, teasing her to take one quick lick.

"Do you want kids?" asked Craig. "Not only Teag and Kitty, but biological ones, too. We love the twins as much as our own, but we'd still love to have you pregnant."

She let out a long, slow breath as Craig took a tube of lube out of his pocket. With a glance filled with sin, he shoved his jeans to the floor. His cock, just as wonderful as his friend's, bounced with his movements.

"So you want me pregnant and barefoot?"

"If you want. Stay at home with the kids or work. It's up to you." Marrick crawled onto the bed, coming up one side of her. "Maybe Curtis will give you a job. He owns Roar."

"Oh. I assumed Purdy owned the place. Besides, something tells me Purdy doesn't like to share his spot behind the bar." She bit her lower lip and reached out for Marrick, but he leaned back, avoiding her.

"Nope. Curtis Podgens is the owner. If he hires you, Purdy has to make room for you."

"Can we stop talking about other men and get to this?" complained Craig. The bed dipped his way as he got on the other side of her.

"You're right, man." Marrick grabbed her jeans and yanked.

She let out a surprised yelp. Her jeans and panties were gone in a flash, leaving her with only her bra. Craig leaned over her. Then with a wicked grin, he took hold of the material with his teeth and tore it away.

"Come here, baby." Marrick took hold of her behind the neck, pulling her forward. He moved as he did, taking her to the edge of the bed. Wrapping his arms around her, he brought her nipple to his mouth and rammed her crotch against his.

His cock, bigger, thicker than before, pressed against her stomach. Flutters of need erupted inside her as she locked her hands around his neck. "Please, Marrick."

"No problem, baby." His fingers dove between her pussy lips. "Are you wet for us?" He grinned and answered his question. "Hell, yeah, you are. You're sopping my hand with your juices."

"Move aside, man. I need a taste of her." Craig pushed against the inside of her legs. "Spread 'em, babe."

She clung to Marrick as she rocked back and forth, moving her legs apart. Although she sensed what Craig had in mind, it still surprised her when he put his head between her legs and his mouth to her pussy. Gone was the gray in his eyes, replaced with flashing amber, as he stared up at her.

She sucked in a quick breath as Craig's tongue took up where Marrick's fingers had left off. But he wasn't satisfied with only his tongue. He plunged his fingers into her pussy as he sucked and nibbled on her clit.

She trembled in a rush of passion. Heat, an accompaniment to the sizzle already searing through her, whipped her passion higher. She leaned back, luxuriating in the feel of Marrick's hands and tongue torturing her nipples and Craig wreaking havoc to her pussy. She pushed against Marrick harder, trapping his cock between her stomach and his.

In and around her clit, Craig worked his magic. His fingers dipped into her sheath, driving into her with a force that would mimic his cock's. A chuckle flowed over her pussy as he brought his other hand to her asshole. She squirmed, the sensation of being filled from both sides overwhelming her. A coolness struck the puckered lips around her anus as Craig made use of the lube.

Marrick's low groan gave way to a purr as he slid his tongue over her breast and up to her throat. She leaned her head back. Would he bite her? Was that what would happen when they changed her? All at once she had her answer. She'd become like them. She'd become a weretiger.

She whimpered as Craig drove fingers from both hands inside her body. He sucked hard, clenching her clit between his teeth. Lust roared into her, taking her by storm and leaving her body shaking in its aftermath.

"Fuck. Now."

If she hadn't been so close to a climax, she would've laughed at Craig's shout of protest as Marrick hoisted her off the bed and away from his friend. With the ease of lifting a small child, he put her on her back.

Would they shift even though they said they wouldn't? Should she be afraid?

"Guys?"

"Don't worry, baby." Marrick shoved Craig aside. "You're safe with me."

He was enormous as he rested on his heels, took her legs with his huge hands, and tugged her toward him. With another growl morphing into a groan, he thrust his cock inside her pussy.

She cried out then slapped a hand over her mouth. *Damn it. Don't wake up the kids.*

Marrick was a machine made of flesh and bones. He rammed into her time and time again, rocking her body.

Craig cupped her breasts and lavished them with kisses. He nipped at her tits, pulling on them. "You're beautiful. Perfect. We couldn't have asked for a better mate."

Did he really expect her to speak? At best, she'd manage a one-word response. Instead, she took him by the arm and met his gaze, putting all her love into one look.

And love it was. Her heart threatened to burst. How could she ever tell them? Language didn't have enough words to say exactly how she felt. Her body was telling them the only way it knew how, but would it be enough? In a rush of emotions, tears flooded her eyes.

Marrick froze, a stunned expression on his face. "What's wrong?"

Craig tenderly took her chin and brought her blurred gaze to his. "Are we hurting you? You have to tell us if we're hurting you. Sometimes—"

"Shut up and let her talk."

She smiled through the tears. "No. It just hit me right then. I mean, I knew it before, but not like I do now."

"What, baby?"

If she hadn't already had tears in her eyes, the worry in Marrick's eyes would've have brought them. "I love you so much. All I want in the world is you two and the twins."

At once, relief flooded their faces.

"So we're not hurting you?" asked Craig.

"No. It's great." She smiled and began working her hips, encouraging Marrick to start making love to her again. "Don't worry. I'll let you know if you ever get too rough."

"Good to know since I wanted to do this."

Marrick jerked her body upward, putting her legs over his shoulders. She gasped as she was positioned with her lower torso higher than the rest of her. Spreading her butt cheeks apart, he slammed his cock deep inside her asshole.

It hurt as he plunged again and again into her. And yet the pain was good, sending her zings of a strange, new kind of pleasure through her.

"Take it easy, babe." Craig fondled her bouncing breasts, playing with her nipples as he watched his friend take her. "If it hurts too much, then say so."

She held on to him for support as Marrick forced each breath from her. Marrick rocked back and forth, thrusting into her, spreading her protesting anus to his will. His amber-brightened gaze met hers as he pressed his thumb to her clit and pushed his fingers into her pussy.

She cried out as the climax surprised her, sending roll after roll of release. Her body was no longer hers. Instead, it had become a servant to her men's needs.

Pleasure transitioned into painful delight. She squirmed, at once fighting to get away, yet wanting to stay. She mewled and reached out for Craig and Marrick.

"Oh, my God," she whispered.

Marrick tensed, his body stiffening even more. Digging his fingers into her hips, he ground out his orgasm as quietly as he could.

He pulled out and shot his cum onto her stomach. Although he wasn't inside her, she still rejoiced in claiming a part of him.

"Move." Craig took her under the arms and pulled her away from Marrick. His friend slid down, coming to rest on his side.

Drawing her close, Craig rested her leg on top of his then, with a quick lick of her nipple, he shoved his cock inside her pussy.

She would've thought she'd be ready for him, prepared by Marrick's lovemaking, but she was wrong. Craig's cock filled her, stretching her wide as he drove deep inside her. His hand cupped her ass cheek and his mouth found her tit again. His pants matched hers as he set up a hard, pounding rhythm.

Their gazes locked, sending each other silent messages of love. His mouth, like hers, parted, the warmth of his breaths meeting hers.

They moved as one, as though they'd been made for each other just as she and Marrick had fit.

The swirling emotions of before joined together with the rush of her body's sensations. They each paused, telling the other their release was close. She saw his climax as hers ripped her apart. Clutching each other, they moaned through their orgasms with soft muted sounds of passion.

When Craig rolled off her, Marrick moved into place at her other side. No one spoke. What need was there for talk? Instead, she lay between her men and listened to their breathing.

I'm home. For now and forever, I'm home.

* * * *

Lisa couldn't imagine being any happier. Not only was she in love, but she had a new home. Even when her boss had called last night and fired her, she hadn't been upset. Why should she? She'd planned on calling him to quit anyway.

She stretched and luxuriated in the coolness of the bed sheets. Craig and Marrick had slipped out earlier to catch up on chores around the ranch. They'd kissed her good-bye, both planting a sweet peck on her cheeks at the same time. They'd told her they loved her and to sleep in.

"Teagie, hurry up!"

Kitty? What are the kids doing up so early?

The twins usually slept late and when they woke up, they immediately started asking for breakfast. Like their uncles, they ate like horses. They'd never go outside until after they'd had a full plate—sometimes even a second helping—of bacon, eggs, and toast along with a huge glass of milk.

She threw off the cover and hurried to the window. Kitty had Teag by the hand and was racing toward the same trees where she'd talked to John Bask.

No.

Fear struck her, propelling her into movement. Tossing on an old T-shirt then tugging on a pair of jeans, she rushed out of the bedroom and hurried to the back door. Her breathing came in shallow pants as she burst outside.

"Kitty! Teag! Kids, stop!"

The twins paused, glanced back at her, and then started running.

What are they doing? Why do they keep running from me?

She took off, wishing she'd had time to find her sneakers instead of the sandals she'd hurriedly pulled on.

"Stop! Kitty! Teag! Stop!"

They didn't look back at her again. Instead, they picked up speed, leaving her farther behind.

A stitch hit Lisa's side, but she kept on going. She couldn't let them go into the trees. What if John was waiting, hiding for just such a chance?

Pain stabbed in her side and still she tried to push on. Her breath burned in her throat and her legs ached. Unable to go another step, she bent over, her hands on her knees as she struggled to breathe. "Kids, come back." She doubted they heard her.

"Daddy!"

Teag's shout brought her head up.

Oh, God, no.

A dark silhouette stood a few feet inside the tree line. The man stepped out into the open then spread his arms wide as the kids ran toward him.

John Bask. Her fear had come true.

"No." Why were they going to him? Hadn't Kitty said she didn't want to go with her father? They'd seen what he'd done to their mother and yet, they still wanted to be with him. But she couldn't blame them. Children loved their parents no matter how bad they were.

Lisa pushed herself to get moving again. The pain in her side tore into her and her voice was lost in her panted breaths, keeping her from calling out for help. But she wouldn't give up again.

Please, don't hurt the kids.

She loved them so much. Somehow, while she was falling in love with Craig and Marrick, she'd fallen in love with the twins, too. If their father did anything to harm them, if he took them away, she'd lie down and die.

At last, she had to give up. She turned, hoping to find them again, but they were gone, nowhere to be seen. Exhausted, she fell to her knees.

Marrick. Craig. Please, help.

Several minutes passed until she could get to her feet again and stumble back to the house. She was panting, dragging in short gasps of air by the time she made it into the living room.

"Lisa, what's wrong?" asked Craig.

Thank God.

She glanced up to see the men striding through the front door. They'd come back early.

"We forgot our phones." Marrick grabbed hold of her and pulled her to the couch. "What's wrong? Where are the twins?"

"He…has…them." She sucked in a hard-won breath then turned it loose in a stream of words. "John has the kids."

Chapter Ten

Marrick's tiger roared to the surface. Even if he'd wanted to keep it in check, he couldn't have. The fury was too great to contain. But he didn't want to stop the beast. His inner animal's need to find John Bask and tear him apart was a part of him. A part he welcomed. A part he'd gladly turn free to exact the revenge he so desperately craved.

"Get as many people as you can together and get out here." Craig, his own eyes telling how close his tiger was to getting out, met Marrick's gaze. "Now. We're going after him. Lisa will show you which way we went."

"No. I'm going with you." Lisa paced across to the other side of the kitchen. "I can't stay here. You already told them he was in the trees. I don't need to show them where."

"Stay here." Marrick snarled as he ripped off his shirt. "You'll just get in the way."

"He's right, babe. We don't want to worry about your safety."

"I'm coming with you. It's my fault. I shouldn't have slept in."

Her stubborn streak showed with the lift of her chin. Marrick knew all the arguing in the world wouldn't keep her at home. Although he admired her resolve, he wasn't happy about it.

"That's a bunch of bullshit. He lured the kids outside." Could she understand him? Fangs pushing out teeth didn't make speaking easy.

"Listen to Marrick." Craig yanked off his boots and sent them flying. "You're not to blame."

She shook her head and paced over to the small window above the sink. "I'm going."

"You won't be able to stay up with us," countered Craig.

Marrick shoved his jeans off along with his boots. He didn't bother talking any longer. The words would only come out as growls. Instead, he closed his eyes and gave up the final layer of resistance to the transformation. Pain seared into him, but it was pain he was used to. Pain that didn't hurt anywhere near as much as the pain goring through him for the children. John would pay for killing Donna, but he'd make John's death a slow, agonizing one if he'd hurt the children.

He hit the floor on all fours, turned to see Craig completing his shift, and then bounded out the back door. Lisa's calls for him to hold up went unheeded as he stretched out his powerful legs and raced toward the trees.

Although his cat mind didn't work the same way as his human one did, it locked onto the problem. Emotions and sensations overtook complete sentences. He felt what he was thinking more than actually putting the ideas into any kind of formal structure.

Prey.

He was hunting his prey. Saliva fell from his jaws. His tongue lolled.

Where?

A car?

No.

A house?

No.

He ran through the trees and came out the other side and into a meadow. Grounding to a stop, he lifted his nose to the air and drew in a long, slow breath. A multitude of aromas struck him.

Rabbit.

Feces.

Trees.

Coyote.

Flowers.

He sorted through the scents.

Yes! Man. Weretiger.

Children.

He growled as Craig came to his side and did his own sniff. A snarl rolled out of him. Together, they changed directions, going toward the smells.

Anyone could have seen them. If the council found out they'd shifted in the daytime, out in the open, they'd have hell to pay. But none of that mattered. Only the children, the small weretigers, mattered.

"Wait for me."

Marrick did a circle, snarling as Lisa came running toward them, and dug his claws into the ground. Pride for his mate's courage struck him, but he didn't have time to waste trying to get her to turn back. Tensing his muscles, he was off again with Craig by his side. Her shouts to let her catch up meant nothing.

He and Craig kept running, going as fast as their tigers could go. After traveling several more yards, they paused and again sniffed, picking up scents that were even stronger than before.

Closer now.

With a growl, he led the way toward the sloping hill. If his memory was right, there was an old hunting lean-to near the hill. He'd forgotten it existed until now. He picked up speed and ran toward the shelter.

My prey.

Him.

A man stood at the entrance to the lean-to. As soon as John saw them, he darted inside the small enclosure.

Craig and he pushed their bodies to their limits, taking the hill in short order. They were close, so close, when John reappeared with Teag at his side. The boy squirmed as his sister stood in the shadow of the shelter, tears streaming down her cheeks. John lifted a gun and pressed it to the boy's head.

Marrick skidded to a halt, his claws digging into the hard ground. Craig almost barreled into him as he came to a stop.

"Marrick, change back or I'll blow his head off," ordered John.

He didn't have a choice. As much as his tiger wanted to taste John's blood, he had to think of the children. Marrick let the transformation slide over him. Craig went through his own shift. Soon they stood side by side, sneering at the enemy. Although weretiger children were used to seeing others naked, they tried to cover themselves.

"Let him go, John." The final stages of the shift shuddered through his body.

"They're my kids. Back the fuck off."

He laughed. Where the humor came from, he wasn't sure. It was ludicrous to think he'd let him walk away with the twins. "After you killed their mother? You are one fucked-up asshole."

John's gaze jumped to Craig and back. "I didn't mean to hurt her." His voice cracked.

Did he really think he'd buy the remorseful act? "Oh, sure. You just ran her down and tore—"

He stopped as Kitty let out a small cry. "It's okay, honey. Your father's going to let you and Teag come back home with me. Then he's going to go away. On a business trip." He struggled to lie, but he couldn't bear to tell them the truth.

"Kitty, come to me." Craig held out his arms.

Kitty took a step toward him then turned toward John. "You hurt Mommy. Why did you hurt Mommy, Daddy?"

"I didn't, honey. Just stay where you are. Your uncle and his friend came to say good-bye." John narrowed his eyes. "No one's taking my kids from me."

Teag squirmed, once again trying to get free. "You hurt Mommy. We saw you hurt Mommy."

Pain seared through Marrick. Knowing John had killed his sister was hard enough. Knowing the kids had seen him do it, made it even harder. "Let them go, John. You turn them loose and we'll give you a head's start."

"Listen to him, man," added Craig.

"No. Don't listen to them, John."

Marrick pivoted around to find Lisa striding toward them. Somehow she'd managed to find them. "Go back to the house, Lisa."

"No. I won't. You can't make me. Not any longer." She moved toward John. "Please. You've got to help me. They've kept me with them, forcing me to stay."

Marrick gawked at her. What was she doing? "Lisa." He couldn't find any other words.

She kept moving closer to the killer. "They said they'd hurt the children if I didn't stay. They said I was their mate." She crossed her arms as though trying to warm herself. "Can you believe that? Me? Letting these two touch me?"

John studied her, obviously trying to understand. "Why should I believe you?"

She paused, an incredulous look on her face. "I didn't tell them that I saw you. I protected you. Now I need you to protect me."

"I don't know…" John frowned, obviously unsure what to think.

"You have to believe me. If you don't, they're going to make me theirs. Please, you've got to save me. Let me come with you and the kids. They love me, don't you, kids?"

John's heated gaze slid over her body. "Kitty, do you like this woman?"

"Uh-huh," whispered Kitty. "Teagie does, too."

"Are you fucking kidding me?" Craig moved toward Lisa. "Babe, what are you doing?"

"Stay away from me." Lisa hurried over to stand near John. She pulled the children close, turning them away from Craig and Marrick. "Don't ever touch me again. I hate you. I hate both of you."

* * * *

Lisa's heart broke to say those words. Marrick's and Craig's hurt tore at her. She wanted to soothe their furrowed brows and wipe away the pain on their faces, but she had to keep going. When she'd come up the slope and seen them, she'd recognized their standoff.

"I hate you." She added all the vehemence she could muster then relaxed her hateful expression. "But I love the children. Please, John, take me with you."

She was winning him over. His eyes had darkened, only the bits of amber brightening as he slid his lustful gaze over her.

"You'd come with me? You'd take care of the kids?"

Lisa held back a curse as Teag struggled to get free. "Yes. I can take you back to my home. They don't know where that is. Or we can go wherever you want. I have enough money to get us by for a year or two. We can make a life together. Just you, me, and the twins."

"Do you know what they are?" John waved the gun toward Marrick and Craig. "What the rest of us are?"

"I know." She licked her lips, drawing his attention. "I wasn't sure if Teag and Kitty knew."

He laughed, the sound hard to her ears. "They do now."

"Good." She turned the children loose and moved closer, getting within a foot of him and the large branch on the ground. If her plan didn't work…

She shoved the awful idea away. It had to work. "They sicken me. I've been watching them hunt for you and getting nowhere." As much as it made her cringe, she slipped her hand along his shoulder. "I want a real man. A real tiger. One who does whatever he wants."

She could feel him straighten to his full height. The man had an ego and she'd just stroked it.

"Lisa, stop it." Marrick's tone was tortured.

"Babe, you can't do this." Craig's eyes pleaded with her.

She ignored them. "There's just one thing."

"What's that?" asked John.

She nodded at Teag. "He has to stop biting." She zeroed in on the small boy, hoping he'd catch her silent meaning. "Do you hear me, Teag? No. More. *Biting*."

Holding her breath, she got ready to act in case the boy understood her. Sure enough, as he had done so many times before, he took her words as a challenge. Opening his mouth wide, he grabbed his father's arm and bit down.

"Shit!" John turned Teag loose.

Lisa snatched up the branch as fast as she could. She brought it up in a wide arc with as every ounce of strength in her. Although she'd aimed for John's head, she connected with the back of his neck.

John let out another howl of pain as Craig and Marrick jumped on top of him. She was knocked out of the way. Scrambling to her feet, she took hold of Teag and Kitty then began pulling them down the slope.

"Go, kids!" She pushed them ahead of her, knowing they could go a lot faster without her. "Run to the house and go to your room. Lock the door behind you. Don't come out unless it's me or one of your uncles."

Thankfully, the children heeded her and took off running. She turned back. Craig and Marrick stood over John who lay on the ground unmoving.

"Baby, keep moving. Watch over the kids until we get back," ordered Marrick.

She didn't want to leave them, but the children needed her more. "Be careful."

"It's almost over," said Craig. "Go on."

She nodded then spun around and started running. By the time she was halfway back to the house, Purdy, Marvin, and a couple of other men she'd seen around town were rushing toward the slope. She bent over, her hands on her knees, trying to catch her breath.

"Where are they?" Purdy leaned over to search her face.

"There." She pointed in the direction she'd come from. "The kids?"

"They should be back at the house by now. Are you going to be okay?"

"I'm fine. Go. They've got John."

The men took off running. She stayed where she was, gulping in replenishing drags of much needed air. When she was finally able, she started toward the house again.

* * * *

Lisa was up and on her feet, moving toward Craig and Marrick when they came through the front door. After getting John Bask into town, the pride's council had been called together for an emergency meeting. Although she'd wanted to go with them, she'd promised to stay with Teag and Kitty and wait for their return. The kids took a while to settle down after what they'd gone through with their father, but she'd finally gotten the twins engrossed in their favorite movie.

Marrick and Craig stalked in and dropped to the couch. Their faces looked haggard as though they'd aged several years in the time they'd been gone.

"Is it over?"

"It's over," answered Marrick as he glanced at the kids sitting at the kitchen table. Their movie played on Craig's computer while they ate cookies and milk. "The council exiled John. He won't be able to join another pride anywhere in the world."

"They let him go?" How could they? He'd murdered his wife. "That's all the punishment he gets?" She lowered her voice. "I don't want to sound mean, but he deserves so much more. He killed your sister and left his poor kids without their mother."

Marrick's jaw clenched and he cast his gaze down. A low rumble of a growl came out of him.

Craig leaned closer. "Weretigers don't kill each other except when there's no other way. We don't have the death penalty even if we would've liked one."

Marrick scoffed. "Yeah, that's the official line. Most of the time, when we seek justice, we get justice."

"What does that mean?" she asked.

"It means I should've killed him when I had the chance. Instead, I let the others haul him before the council."

She checked Craig and saw that he felt the same way. "Then why didn't you?"

A small smile played on Marrick's lips, but it held no real joy. "Because I was stupid. And too slow to act."

"So John is exiled. Big deal."

"Actually, it is a big deal." Craig took the small glass bowl off the coffee table and worked it around in his hands as though he simply needed something to do. "Weretigers are like a lot of other cats. We like solitude, but at the same time, we want to be part of a pride. As an exile, John won't have any pride to take his back. That leaves him vulnerable to a lot of other shifters."

"If we're lucky, the werewolves will get him." Marrick grim smile grew.

"Werewolves? So they exist, too? What about vampires?"

"All of it," answered Craig. "Wherever he goes, he'll be in danger. If another group of shifters finds out he's alone, he becomes an easy target."

"Especially since I'll spread the word that he's out of our pride."

"So he's a dead man walking? Is that what you're saying?" A shiver ran through her. Exile might prove worse than any death penalty.

"Yeah. He is."

"And what about you? What did the council say about you shifting during the day?"

"Under the circumstances, they decided they'd let it pass this time." Marrick groaned and worked his neck around.

Craig stood, letting out a huge sigh. "It's over and I'm starving. How about I fix us some dinner?"

"There's soup on top of the stove." She motioned to the kids. "Teag and Kitty already ate their dinner."

She'd fixed dinner, knowing the men could use some comfort food, but also hoping the children would go to bed early. Even if they didn't feel up to sex, she wanted to comfort them in any way she could.

"Sounds good." The laugh lines around Craig's eyes crinkled together. "Babe, what you did, whacking John and all, was amazing. You saved the kids and maybe our lives."

"I had to do something."

"You sure had us fooled. For a minute, I thought you were serious about leaving with him."

Shrugging, she downplayed his praise. "But only for a minute, huh?"

"Yeah. You had me convinced until you said you had money." Craig scoffed. "When you said that, then I knew you were lying."

"I was hoping you'd catch on."

"Like I said. You were amazing." Craig's stomach grumbled. "I'm ready for some grub. Marrick?"

"I'll get some in a while." Marrick slicked his fingers through his hair and slumped down.

"Are you going to be okay?"

He didn't look at her. "I will be. Later."

She wasn't sure what else she could say or do. "If you need anything…" Standing, she yelped when he snagged her by the arm.

"Tell me you're staying. For good. For us and the kids. Tell me."

Her breath hitched in her throat. He'd never sounded so vulnerable. "Yes. I'm staying for as long as you want me. For a lifetime, if that's what you want."

"That's what we all want." He moved to caress the curve of her hip. "That's what we all need."

"Then that's what I'll do." She leaned over and placed a kiss on top of his head. "Let me fix you a bowl."

Moving to the kitchen, she couldn't help but smile. She'd made her decision. They were her men and her children now.

Epilogue

Feeling naughty, Lisa dove under the covers. As had become their habit—as long as they remembered to lock the bedroom door—she, Craig, and Marrick had gone to bed naked. Why bother with a nightie when it would get torn off her as soon they got into bed?

Her hand encircled Craig's cock as she scooted over closer to Marrick. Flicking her tongue over his cock, she slid it into her mouth. A smile came as the men awakened from her touch.

"Holy shit." Craig gripped the bedspread.

"Fucking yeah." Marrick's hands tunneled into her hair.

In and out she pulled Marrick's cock. Up and down she slid her palm over Craig's shaft. Within a minute, both men were hard and throbbing. They moaned their delights, accented with an occasional growl.

She switched, taking Craig's cock into her mouth while her hand cupped Marrick's balls. Lying across Craig's leg, she rocked back and forth, rubbing her breasts against him. He moaned again and put his hands in her hair as Marrick had done.

Pumping, sucking, she worked them, showing them her love. She'd adored them before, but after having lived with them for the past month, she'd grown to love them more than she would've ever believed it possible to love anyone. How had she lived before finding them? She'd gained not only two amazing, sexy, caring men, but she'd become part of a family.

Shoot. The kids will be up soon.

She quickened her pace, rolling her tongue over Craig's length as she picked up speed with Marrick's cock. They'd spread their legs, giving her access, but also an invitation.

Which one to ride?

She'd learned their likes and knew both of them enjoyed having her on top. Trying to remember which one she'd ridden yesterday, she decided to just go for it. Why worry when she'd end up riding them both anyway?

She flicked her tongue over the end of Craig's in a good-bye, and then crawled on top of Marrick. He threw off the cover, gripped her by the waist, and hoisted her over his cock.

"Damn it, babe. I needed you first today," complained Craig.

"No more than I did." Marrick's gaze met hers as he slid his huge cock inside her.

The feel of him stretching her vaginal walls had her laying her head back and sighing. Her breasts bounced with each of his thrusts until he caught them and began massaging her nipples.

Craig got onto his knees and nibbled on her neck. "Make it short and sweet. I want my turn."

Her hair played around her face. Flattening her hands against Marrick's chest, she leaned forward, prompting his cock to skim over her G-spot. The muscles in his chest rippled as he fondled her tits and pounded his cock into her.

His only complaint was when Craig pried his hands off her breasts. His friend chuckled then claimed them for his own.

"Is this the day, baby?" Marrick had a strange habit of talking while he made love.

"The day you change me?" Her breath was ragged, making it difficult to talk.

"Yeah," murmured Craig with his lips to the curve of her shoulder. He tweaked her nipples then slicked his tongue along her skin. "You said you wanted to be a shifter."

"I do, but not today."

She didn't expand on her answer. It wasn't as though they hadn't talked enough about it already. As she'd explained to them, she wanted to wait until Teag and Kitty started school. Having them in school would give her more time to adjust to life as a weretigress without having to worry about watching over them.

"Okay. We're ready whenever you are."

Craig moved behind her. "I'm coming in the back way, babe."

She laughed and bent forward, pushing out her butt. A coolness hit her anus as Craig lubricated her, preparing her. More times than not, he'd opted for taking her from behind and she loved it. Somehow it seemed more primal, more...tiger-like.

Still, she was unprepared as he slammed his thighs against the backs of her legs and shoved his cock inside her ass. Pain hit her, but didn't last long. Instead, the pleasure Marrick was giving her flowed over to her butt hole as Craig set up a rhythm to match his friend's.

"We've caught you now."

Although she didn't say so, she knew he was wrong. She was the one who'd caught them. A giggle escaped her.

I caught two tigers.

"What's so funny?"

Marrick barely got the word about before a growl rolled out of him. He paused, then with a low roar, he plunged into her again. His climax broke from him, shuddering his body under hers.

She tightened her hold around his cock. Hot semen flowed into her. Although it would take time for the birth control pills to wear off, she couldn't help but hope he'd planted their first child inside her.

"Fuck. Too short." Craig gripped her hips and pulled her back hard and fast. He paused, then with a roar that mimicked Marrick's, he pulled out of her and let his release go.

Her climax came on the heels of his, storming through her, taking both her mind and her body. She smothered her cry and fell on top of Marrick. Craig, his body still shaking, dropped to her side.

They stayed still, enjoying the after-effects of their lovemaking. She listened, knowing it wouldn't be long before the twins were up and running.

"We love you."

The words were so simple, and yet the way Marrick said them made them sound like music.

"I love you, too." As it always did, the idea of having found them gave her a rush of joy.

"I know we've talked about this before, but—"

She interrupted Craig, answering before he could ask. It was as if they needed reassurance every day. "Yes, I'm staying. I'm your mate and your mine. And yes, I do want to change into a weretiger later. And yes, I do want kids of our own. Not that I could ever love them any more than I do Teag and Kitty. As for working, I think I'll have enough to handle raising our kids."

Marrick's chest rose and fell with a heavy sigh. "Like I said before, we're ready whenever you are."

"Good." She sat up and listened, hearing the voices of the children. "They're up. Better get dressed, you two."

"You get dressed," ordered Craig.

She slapped his hands as she crawled over him to get out of the bed. "Oh, really? Are you planning on staying in bed all day?"

"Nope." Marrick was on his feet as Craig got out of the bed behind her.

She threw on a T-shirt and yanked on her jeans. "What's going on?"

Craig's image started blurring. Bones began breaking.

"Why is Craig shifting?"

"Because, baby, now that we're sure the twins know about weretigers, we've decided it's time to play a little game called Catch a Tiger by the Tail."

"And how's that played?" She started toward the bedroom door as Marrick turned his tiger loose.

"Easy." His words were garbled. "You and the twins chase us. If you can catch us by the tail, you win."

"You're not supposed to shift during the day, remember?"

"Then we can't let anyone see us. Come on. Be daring, baby." Marrick's transformation sped up.

In under a minute, both men had changed.

They're so amazing. As men and as tigers.

Lisa flung open the bedroom door. "Hey, kids. Want to play a game?"

Marrick and Craig dashed past her, heading toward the stairs. Teag and Kitty burst out of their bedroom and into the hall.

"A game?" asked an excited Kitty.

"A really fun game." Lisa pointed toward the stairs as Marrick and Craig darted down them. "It's called Catch a Tiger by the Tail. If you win, we'll go to town and get ice cream."

"Yay!" Teag sprinted down the hallway.

Kitty, however, threw her body against Lisa's. "I love you."

Tears sprang to Lisa's eyes. "I love you, too, sweetie." She took Kitty's arms and eased her back. "Now how about we catch a tiger by the tail?"

She laughed, happy and fulfilled, as Kitty ran after her brother.

THE END

WWW.JANEJAMISON.COM

ABOUT THE AUTHOR

Jane Jamison has always liked "weird stuff" as her mother called it. From an early age she was fascinated with stories about werewolves, vampires, space, aliens, and whatever was hiding in her bedroom closet. To this day, she still swears she can hear growls and moans whenever the lights are out.

Being born under the sign of Scorpio meant Jane was destined to be very sensual. Some would say she was, and remains, downright sexual. Then one day she put her two favorite things together on paper and found her life's true ambition—to be an erotic paranormal romance author.

Jane spends her days in her office surrounded by the characters she loves. Often a new character will knock on the door of her imagination and spark the idea for another book.

Her future includes traveling, learning the art of photography, traveling, and writing more books. Thanks to her loving husband, she continues to turn her dreams into realities.

For all titles by Jane Jamison, please visit
www.bookstrand.com/jane-jamison

Siren Publishing, Inc.
www.SirenPublishing.com

Lightning Source UK Ltd.
Milton Keynes UK
UKOW06f1854240216

269070UK00015B/296/P